PRAISE FOR DUNCAN B. BARLOW

Labyrinthine, lyrical, and provocative, *The City, Awake* is part philosophical mystery, part dream-like meditation on what it means to be human, all wrapped up into a beguiling postmodern puzzle. Buttressed by Barlow's luminous prose, *The City, Awake* takes us on an astonishing journey through the darkened bars and hidden alleyways of an expertly-constructed, claustrophobic cityscape where hitmen are sometimes helpless, where femme fatales are seldom what they seem, and where grit and the angelic mingle on every page —a gorgeous surprise.

— McCORMICK TEMPLEMAN

In Barlow's Cincinnati-gone-strange, a germ-obsessed electrified man finds himself at the mercy of a mutant cat man, an odd doctor, misguided policemen, and (perhaps worst of all) the terrors of dating. Unrelentingly bizarre and mysterious, unsettling in all the right ways, *Super Cell Anemia* is a strange and powerful debut.

—BRIAN EVENSON

Of Flesh and Fur is an ancient fable that comes from the not too distant future. Its fevered coyotes worry the bones of fathers who don't have sons, of those who are abandoned and abandon in turn. There's only hunger in these pages, fantasies of manliness that make thin feed. Barlow's spare prose spares us nothing. Read or be eaten.

— JOANNA RUOCCO

Prepare yourself, good reader, for you are about to have the great fortune of meeting Gilles, dreamer of dark and beautiful dreams, spinner of strange syntax, copper biter, spark shooter, cat chaser, tunnel explorer, vigilant neighbor and, most importantly, hero of this knockout novel. Go ahead, try it, see for yourself (the guy, like the book, is high-voltage) — shake his hand…

—LAIRD HUNT

acknowledgments

James Reich and Stalking Horse Press, Valerie and Scout Barlow, Montelle Mansfield, Brian Evenson, Brian Kiteley, Chris Narozny, Tobias Carroll, Derek White, Lee Ann Roripaugh, Andy Tinsley, Robert Pennington, Nicole Suazo, Moon River pizza for providing a place for me to write when I needed an escape, the faculty and students at University of South Dakota for their patience during the final editing stage of this novel, and finally, McCormick Templeman, David Gruber, Laird Hunt, and Marthine Satris for insightful commentary on the early versions of this novel.

THE CITY, AWAKE

ALSO BY DUNCAN B. BARLOW

Of Flesh and Fur

Super Cell Anemia

duncan b. barlow

THE CITY, AWAKE

Stalking Horse Press
Santa Fe, New Mexico

THE CITY, AWAKE

Copyright © 2016 by duncan b. barlow
ISBN: 978-0-9984339-0-5
Library of Congress Control Number: 2016961088

First paperback edition published by Stalking Horse Press, March 2017

The characters and events in this book are fictitious. Any similarity to real persons, living or dead, is coincidental and not intended by the author.

www.stalkinghorsepress.com

Photograph and Design by James Reich
Inside Art Credit: S. Fisher Williams at Aqua Lab Studios

Stalking Horse Press
Santa Fe, New Mexico

Stalking Horse Press requests that authors designate a nonprofit, charitable, or humanitarian organization to receive a portion of revenue from the sales of each title. duncan b. barlow has chosen the American Indian College Fund. www.collegefund.org

For the Noltemeyer Family

THE CITY, AWAKE

So it must necessarily follow that Nature, which results from no causes, and which we nevertheless know to exist, must necessarily be a perfect being to which existence belongs.

—*Baruch Spinoza*

18

HE AWOKE in his bed, fully clothed. In his right pocket, a note that read, *You are David. You were made in God's image. You are the author of all language, emender of sins.*

HE STOOD and regarded himself in the mirror. His black slacks and white oxford were remarkably smooth for having slept in them. His head buzzed, yet he couldn't remember drinking. He didn't remember much of anything. He was unsure if he truly was David or if this message was intended for someone else. The bedroom was tidy, nothing out of place, not that there was much to it, a thin table with a small drawer, a twin-sized bed, white sheets, a brass lamp, and a black rotary phone. An abstract painting of a full moon hovering over the sea hung above the bed. David leaned in to look at it. The brush strokes were angry, scraped across the canvas as if the artist's hand had been forced, in sharp contrast to the serenity depicted. The living room was no more lavish. A brown leather couch, a matching chair, one standing brass lamp, and a book of matches with *Smathers' Bar* embossed upon it. There was something to the matches that compelled him to pick them up. Some unformed thought. In blue pen, *Box 316 Union Station* was written on the inside. Had he written this? He sat on the edge of the couch and ran his fingers through his hair. The viscous pomade stuck to him. It reeked of mineral oil.

Words formed in his head. Although he could not remember how he knew the names of the items of which he took catalogue, he was certain of their function and sign. Putting the pack of matches into his right pocket, he grabbed the glass doorknob to leave. The crown of it was coarse upon his palm. Closing the door behind him, David made note of his room number. He traveled down a dimly lit hallway with a seemingly endless number of doors just like his and descended the stairs. In the lobby, a feeble old man in an undershirt and brown dress slacks sat with his back to the service window. A clock radio broadcasted a boxing match at a knifing volume. A man named The Irish Hammer had another sap backed into a corner. He pounded him without mercy.

"Where is—"

The old man pointed north. His hand was thin and crawling with veins. It looked alien next to the smooth ivory and gold flecked shell of the clock radio.

"You don't know what I was going to ask."

The old man pulled his finger to his lips and shushed him. A bell rang and the sports commentators launched into a conversation about denture powder. The gaunt man turned his attention to the front of the desk and said, "Smathers' is to the left and down the street." He waved his hand dismissively and returned his focus to the radio speaker, turning the clear plastic volume knob up even farther.

The night sky, low with cloud, threatened to snuff out what feeble streetlights hadn't burned out long before. The wet sidewalk reflected the blinking hotel sign, a cursive, red neon: Hotel South. Despite the rain, the air was hot. It clung to his shirt, a spider web heavy with dew. His black wingtips trundled against the concrete as he walked to find Smathers'. The old man's directions did not wrong him. The bar was two blocks north.

A young black man played piano on a decrepit upright, pushed in the back of the smoky bar. Through the gloom, the bottles of alcohol glistened like jewels. David took a seat on a vacant stool. As he surveyed the room, the barkeep placed a bourbon between his hands.

"I haven't made up my mind yet."

"Listen to that, Rudy. David ain't made up his mind yet." The bartender said, "You always drink the same thing."

"How'd you know to call me David?"

"It's your name, ain't it?"

David examined himself in the dingy mirror behind the bottles. The sharp cut of his jaw, the brush of shadow in the faint clef of his chin, the thinness of his lips. It was the face of a stranger that he could only place through the contextual clues of movement. It seemed the short, bald man behind the counter knew him well enough. However, he didn't necessarily feel like a David. He rolled the glass between his hands. No ice. Straight up. He could remember the word *bourbon* and he could connect the name with the object, but he couldn't remember ever having tasted it before. He lifted the glass and took a small sip. The amber liquid cut through his throat like paint thinner. It burned and tasted something awful. He couldn't be David because he didn't like bourbon. At the bottom of the glass, the dim yellow lights swam, blond eels chewing at each other's caudal fins.

The warped voice of a woman came to him as if in a dream.

He closed his eyes. Focused.

Remain, she said, so faintly that he could barely decipher the voice in his own thoughts.

"Remain," he said aloud.

The bartender came back, leaned toward him, and said, "What's that, David?"

"I said nothing."

"You're acting funny tonight." The small man walked down the bar and talked to Rudy.

Again, the voice of the woman whispered, so musical this time that it seemed to come from the harp of the piano. *Saul*, it said.

The name felt familiar, much the way the word *chair* or *table* felt inside his head, like an old memory, only stronger and because of this, he assumed this to be his name and summarily adopted it. Saul looked around the bar. Perhaps the voice was not inside him, but came from elsewhere, a booth, a corner, some construct that projected sound. Each booth was occupied by lonely men drinking away their miseries. Saul surveyed the room three times and then slowly began backing toward the door. It was only, however, a few steps into his retreat that he bumped into someone.

"A man of your stature should watch where he's going if he knows what's good for him."

"Pardon."

"I suspect you're going to offer a drink to the girl you just trampled."

"I suppose so."

She slipped through the air like a ghost and found a seat at the bar. Saul took the stool to her right and signaled for two drinks. The barkeep slid another fifth of brown liquor to Saul, and in front of the woman, he placed a slender glass, which blossomed into an Elizabethan collar at the top. Her slender fingers stroked the stem. The word *martini* formed in Saul's mind.

"You're clueless."

He angled his head and stared at her. "Do you always start conversations with insults?"

She smiled, her plum lips rising over her teeth like an eyelid. "Only now," she said. "It fits."

She uncased a cigarette, put it in her mouth. His hand instinctively reached inside his pocket and removed the matches. Striking the head against the friction strip, Saul lit the match and cupped the flame.

The woman released a silent, smoky whistle and said, "Right now, you're wondering how you knew to do that."

"I'm sorry," he said as if asking a question, and she repeated herself. He had, in fact, just wondered why he had lit her smoke. However, that thought was quickly replaced with the question of how she knew.

"Are you following me?"

"Don't ask questions," she whispered into his ear. "It's a sign of weakness. At this moment, you can't afford to look weak."

She ran her finger along the edge of his chin and quickly turned away to watch the piano player as he launched into an old stride classic. Saul's drink glistened beneath the dim light.

"We should leave," she said.

"Who are you?" he asked.

"What did I say about questions?"

"Tell me your name."

"Much better," she smiled, pulling a small clutch purse into her hand. "Merav. Now let's go."

Saul followed Merav. His gaze fell to her waist, which moved in her dress like a dreaming serpent. She led him through the dim narrow streets of the city, each street seeming to vanish behind them. Small puddles reflected the moonlight and broke it into rings as they stepped. After several blocks, Saul grabbed Merav's wrist and pulled her to him.

"Tell me why I'm following you."

"Inquiry."

"Merav, you don't know me as well as you think you do."

"Then how did I find you?" she asked, kissing his cheek.

The backstreet was busy only with shadows crawling away from the moonlight and hiding in corners and gutters. Merav's sharp heels clicked through the streets, ricocheting between faceless buildings. If he'd known anything, he'd thought he'd known better. But as this world unfolded before him like some dying carnation, he in the folds of its willing petals, he figured following someone as lovely as Merav would be as good an end as any.

1

HE AWOKE in his bed, fully clothed. In his right pocket, he found a note that read, *You are David. You were made in God's image. You are the author of all language, emender of sins.*

DAVID STOOD and regarded himself in the mirror. He extended his arm and watched his hand as he opened and closed it. God is wonderful, he thought, I am special. Stepping into the living room, David smoothed the folds in his hair, smiling at the tacky resistance of his pomade. He walked along the hallway, surprised by the length of it. As he navigated through the gloom, it dawned on him that he had forgotten to check his room number. He walked back and guessed at a few doors before finally finding the lock that fit his key. "Seven Twenty," he whispered as he patted his pockets.

When he arrived at the service desk, he stood quietly and waited for the attendant to turn his attention away from the radio and assist him. Patience, after all, was a virtue. When the novelty of his virtue began to wear thin, David rang the bell. The old man said, "Smathers' is down the street." Although David did not know why the old man had said this, he took it as a sign from God and left the building in search for Smathers'.

At the bar, David bellied up and the barkeep said, "Back so

soon, David?" He slid a bourbon to him and David quickly took a sip. A bit intense, he thought, but good. He nursed the drink for a while before a short man with white hair sat at his side.

"David, you're late."

David smiled and said, "Patience is a virtue."

The small man frowned and said, "Join me outside, will you?"

23

ACROSS THE street, two men walked out of the bar. One brought the other closer to him. It began to rain. David looked up for less than a second. When he returned his gaze, only one man remained and the rain ceased. He tried to find where the taller of the two men had gone, but there was no trace, as if the rain had come to wash him from Earth.

The cold began to creep deeper into him. The days were manageable. Even in the winter, he felt the sun on his skin. However, nights were cold and windy and run through with vermin. David pulled his collar up around his ears and leaned into a cranny behind a dumpster. If there had been summers where he'd felt warm, he couldn't remember.

David pulled a few more bundles of newsprint into his hands and shoved them under his tattered coat. How many days had he been living like this? He looked to his arm. One year, two weeks, three days. With the pen he kept hidden in his pocket, he marked another day. Pulling the sleeve down, he tried to recall how it had all happened.

He remembered waking up, but nothing before that. He was told that his name was David. He had found his way to Smathers', where he had met an old man while drinking. There were dreams too—that is when he was lucky enough to find sleep. No matter where they began, they ended in the same place. A lab. A table. Tubes and wires. A burning chemical. It was violet and clear, a precious jewel glinting. Sometimes there was a man in a lab coat. The man spoke to him in an angry language he did not understand. It sounded like *clothing dry and something*. After these dreams he tried to infer meaning from the words. Switching them around. Jumbling them. But he never found a message, a solution. There were other dreams in which he would turn and see a man next to him. He would try to speak, finding it impossible. Then, the man would face him and David would see the stranger looked just like him. The other would attempt to say something, but blood would pour from his mouth, thick and red.

David peeked around the edge of the trash to watch the bar across the street. No one moved. A man in shirtsleeves walked out and lit a smoke. How could he not feel the cold? David pulled his arms around himself and leaned back into the shadows. Somewhere there was an itch. Some days he felt he could locate it. Other days it was everywhere at once. He shifted inside his papers and used the wall as a scratching pad but found no respite. The streetlight caught a bit of wrist and revealed a small maggot crawling into his flesh.

"It's not there."

David closed his eyes, pressed the lids so tightly together that he felt they might vanish. When he reopened them, the maggot was gone.

18

BEFORE THEY had reached the penthouse suite, Saul and Merav climbed several flights of unlit stairs. The staircase had seemed infinite, constantly curling upon itself. Just when Saul had convinced himself to turn around, Merav had stepped onto a landing and submerged herself into the gloom of the hallway. The sound of Merav's heels had pierced the darkness and he had followed her like a beacon. But she wasn't light. There was nothing luminous about her. Still, he had followed her, as even when they weren't speaking, he'd continued to hear her voice in his head. Whenever he'd thought of turning away, the voice had whispered *follow*, and so he would abide.

IN A grand library, they sat facing each other in prodigious leather chairs. Merav eyed Saul and soon he became uncomfortable.

"You're staring at me."

"No," she replied.

"You most certainly are."

"Perhaps I'm staring *into* you. Perhaps I'm reading you to see if you are the man I think you are."

From behind Saul, came a faint creaking noise, but before

he could turn or speak or stand, there was a prick in his neck—
then the room fell black.

30

He awoke in his bed, fully clothed. In his right pocket, he found a note that read, *You are David. You were made in God's image. You are the author of all language, emender of sins.*

David arose from the bed and took inventory of the room. Bed, table, phone. He opened the drawer to the table and found a Bible and a book of matches with *Smathers'* printed on them. As he looked at the contents of the drawer, David noticed a small red bump in the crook of his elbow. When he touched it, a burning sensation ran up his bicep. He closed the drawer and left the apartment. He learned the room number and made his way out of the building.

When he arrived at Smathers', the barkeep poured a drink and asked, "Thirsty today?"

David said nothing, swilled the drink, and turned his back to the bar.

A small man with silver hair stood and approached him. "David," he said, "my name is Mr. Erelim. We must speak."

David nodded and joined him at a booth removed from the other patrons. Mr. Erelim folded his hands, his lips closed into a tight line, and he reached up and rubbed David's chin. The move had been so quick, the old man was finished before David could react.

"God is truly great," Mr. Erelim said. "Are you able to speak?"

David opened his mouth, felt his tongue move, but found no voice. He shook his head.

"The Lord has blessed you with his greatest gift."

18

SAUL CAME to, the world awash in a Gaussian blur, but soon his focus returned and he found himself facing a closed door. There was a strange warmth in his legs. Though they were slow to respond, he wiggled his thighs against the cushions on a long purple couch. His hands were crossed in his lap and he wondered if should keep them at his sides in case someone were to come through the door and attack him. Why would he worry about being attacked? He remembered he was following a woman. He followed her up from the bar. Then what? He fainted. Yes. No. There was something else. A pinprick. Saul stood up and checked the room. It was dark, a brass lamp revealing the couch, table, and hardwood floor around him. Outside of that, he could only make out faint corners. Perhaps books on shelves. A lot of books. Something resting on a mantle. Something long, reflective. He squinted to manage the darkness. Just as his vision began to blur with moisture, he saw two silver dots move. Saul backed away from the couch.

"Don't be alarmed," a whispering breath called from the gloom.

The silver dots grew and a face emerged, slowly. It looked to float, gliding smoothly from the shadows. A bald man with a skeletal face maneuvered his wheelchair into the light. He fussed with an ill-fitting crimson robe and said, "You're safe here. They won't hurt you again."

Saul turned to open the door, but stopped when the man said, "Don't you want to know who David is?"

Turning around, Saul faced the man, who was now immersed in the golden light of a floor lamp. He was fragile. IVs dangled around his head, angels tethered by tubing.

"I'm listening."

"I'm quite sure you are, Saul. Your curiosity is your second motivational force."

"You seem to know me. Tell me what my first motivation is."

"Ah," the old man whispered through a hole in his throat, "all in due time."

Yes, due time, came a familiar whisper inside his own skull.

Saul looked around but saw no one standing in the room. He placed his finger into his ear, casually. Nothing there. No device.

"Please take a seat," the old man said, his thin hand gesturing toward the couch.

Saul perched on the edge of the cushion, his legs beneath him, ready loaded springs. The old man fussed with a strange remote wired to an arachnid medicine dispenser. The device came to life and one of the legs rose, fell into the man's shoulder, and injected a shot. He leaned his head back for an instant and clicked his dry old tongue against his teeth. A small plume of air came from his trachea and he spoke. "You see, I am a very sick man. It is not too often that I have visitors. My—" He paused, dropped his remote, and began anew, "I have become accustomed to my day-to-day activities and have forgotten how strange they may appear to outsiders."

From a door that opened to another room, a slim woman emerged. She leaned against the jamb, her auburn hair upon her shoulders, and took a long drag from her cigarette. After the smoke eased from her lips, she said, "I trust you've made Saul feel comfortable."

As Saul stared at the woman, his eyes narrowed and then relaxed. Had he followed her into the building? He couldn't remember, but he was certain he'd followed a blond.

"You look surprised to see me, Saul."

Merav took a seat next to the man in the wheelchair. She placed her hand atop his forearm.

"Mr. Uriah, our friend has forgotten me already."

"I followed you here, but something happened. A pain in my neck. A time of blackness."

Mr. Uriah clicked his lips together and said, "I am sorry about that. With Merav out of the room to change, we had to be certain you wouldn't be able to attack me."

"What made you certain that I wouldn't attack you when I woke up?"

"Saul, dear, I told you that questions make you look weak."

"Once I knew that Merav had brought the correct gentleman, I knew it was safe to let you live. I had to make sure you were the right one. After all, you all do look quite similar."

"I don't know what you're talking about, Mr. Uriah."

"All in due time, my boy."

30

DAVID FOLLOWED Mr. Erelim through a series of streets with no names. He made note of landmarks as a way to map his return to the South. There was very little he recognized, but he was filled with a sense of déjà vu. He took catalog: damaged street light, gold lions, broken window second floor. Even through the black of the alleys and thin thoroughfares, David could see the old man's silver hair, as if it had its own lighting filament. At times David wanted to touch it, to feel if it was coarse or soft like his own.

They entered a somber alley and Mr. Erelim jumped to grab the bottom rung of a fire escape. He was remarkably spry for a man of his age. David followed him, finding his own agility surprising. They scaled the ladder until it became a landing and farther still until it became steps. When they arrived at the top floor, Mr. Erelim opened a window and the two crawled in. The old man's feet made no sound, but David's clacked against the hardwood floor. A table lamp came on and Mr. Erelim was already seated in a black leather chair.

"We must talk, David."

David took a seat across from the old man. He trusted him, but didn't understand why. A servant came ambling out of the darkness with two drinks in his hands. As he stretched to deliver the bourbon, David caught a glimpse of what appeared to be pitch skin with a white tattoo.

"We've been waiting a long time for you, David."

David allowed the burn of alcohol to loosen him. He took inventory of the room. Two doors, three windows, a lamp with a chord long enough to strangle the old man.

"There are no mistakes, David. I want you to understand that first."

David nodded.

"In great experiments, every move is part of the grand process." The man took a sip of his drink and paused. "I have a mission for you. I know you'll have questions, but you'll simply have to trust me. I will take care of you, David."

18

SAUL WATCHED the people on the street. He tried his coffee and waited for Merav. The coffee was better with cream. He poured more into the mug. He enjoyed the way the white swirled in the murky water. The cobblestone square was crawling with tourists, all taking in the marvelous architecture of the square with its robust stone buildings, stained black from the elements and smoke of a bygone coal era. Buskers and conmen punctuated the cross traffic, each competing for the spare change lining the pockets of the crowd. A businessman and a courier, hastily navigating the free space, nearly collided into one another, but changed directions mere seconds before impact as if they had choreographed it.

A woman with hair the color of rooibos tea sat at a table across from him and opened a book.

You shouldn't be so vulnerable.

The voice had returned inside his head. Saul bowed and made to look at the watch the old man had given him the previous night. It was a fine Swiss watch, whose gears made very little, if any noise. From his periphery, he examined the area but could not find a woman any closer than the woman with rooibos hair. As he attempted to read the jacket of her hardback, she closed it and walked past, leaving a slip of folded paper on his table. Saul covered it with his hand. When he was sure no one was looking, he read it.

Overbee Hotel.

Saul left a few coins for the waiter and went in search of the Overbee Hotel. He'd not remembered seeing it when following Merav, but they'd turned down so many poorly lit corridors, it was hard to keep track of the landmarks.

The streets were all familiar to him but he couldn't seem to place them. The faces of the people who passed him on the street were all unfamiliar. It stood to reason that he would recognize someone, anyone, but he did not. Every face seemed new to him. He did, after all, remember words, and the names of monuments he couldn't recall seeing before he woke in the hotel. Was this unique to him, he began to wonder, or was this the way the world was? A man wakes up with a slip of paper in his pocket and lives his life. As he yielded for a mother pushing a stroller, he realized how foolish his line of inquiry had been. Of course men weren't born in hotel rooms fully clothed.

After dodging three cabs that he believed went out of their way to displace him, he found himself standing before a large fountain recessed from the sidewalk. Several children played around the monument, which had, through time, become less of a fountain and more of a statue. Saul approached it with a sense of trepidation that he couldn't quite place. In its shadow, he found himself entranced by the baroque angel frozen in battle.

Although they had darkened with age and neglect, the angel's features were visible. Between his eyelids peeked slivers of iris that appeared somehow darker than black. The massive warrior's wings spread to the edge of the drained basin several feet below. One hand reached toward the heavens while the other held a copper sword that no longer glistened in the sunlight. On the edge of the basin was a brass plate, long ago worn flat, which likely contained information about the monument; however, someone had scratched *Repent all ye sinners* crudely upon the metal. Saul felt cold gather in his spine and he shuddered. He shoved his hands into his pockets and continued walking.

It was night by the time he reached the Overbee Hotel. A man received Saul at the entrance and opened the mammoth brass doors. The concierge waved him to the counter and handed him a small piece of paper.

Saul grimaced and said, "You're sure this goes to me?"

The slight man behind the desk smiled, his mustache curling at the ends. "Madame said to give it to the man who looks lost."

Saul opened the slip of paper.

1011

He walked to the elevator, where the operator greeted him. Without another word, the redhead moved a lever. Saul examined the floors as they passed the gated window. Each level seemed to crawl down from the ceiling and reveal itself to them like a secret: lovers kissing at their doorway; young bureaucrats slicking their hair back upon their heads as they left their rooms for meetings; a boy in a sailor suit riding a tricycle between two suites.

When they reached the tenth level, the operator cast his glance to his shoes and said, "Penthouse."

He fumbled with the handle and, when it opened, said, "Have a good day, sir."

It wasn't until Saul stepped out of the lift that he realized that the hallway was submerged in near dark. He turned and said, "This floor has no lights."

"I don't come to this floor," the operator said. "Something about it don't sit right with me."

"But the lights," Saul began.

"They're on, you just have to get used to them. Ring for me when you're done."

He pulled the door shut and Saul watched as the light sank into the floor.

He squinted against the darkness. There was a noise in the distance. A man talking. Saul shuffled his feet in that direction. The blackness seemed to press against him, and as he moved forward, his body felt electric for he knew that he could stumble at any moment.

By the time he'd crept along for a few minutes, his vision had begun to adjust to the low lighting. He reached a set of grand doors nearly three times his height. He pressed his ear against their cool leather padding and struggled to hear over his breath. A voice came into his ear, but he couldn't quite make out what it said. He pushed his weight against the door and inched it forward, easing into a room that would have been completely pitch, had it not been for a retractable ceiling that was open to the humid night air. Saul hid behind a high back chair.

He counted twelve people in the room, maybe thirteen if the very still man wasn't a statue. In the low light their faces look like blank masks, featureless and grim.

Uriah's faint voice rose from somewhere in the room. "The head must be removed. Let us now proceed. As is tradition, please light your candles and hold them aloft."

The men obeyed and for the first time, Saul could make out that each man wore a hooded cloak.

"We are the bearers of light, the harbingers of the new world, sworn to purge Earth of prophets of oppression and fallacy. May our flames serve as a beacon to lead the misguided into the world of knowledge and logic."

In unison, the men said, "Veritatem tantum, et profectus est." Then, each man snuffed his candle out with the palm of his hand and the group filed out a door at the far end of the room.

Wall lamps came to a dim glow to reveal Mr. Uriah sitting in his wheelchair.

"Come sit with me Saul."

Saul stood and joined him.

"How long did you know?"

"Before you even arrived."

From behind the back of the wheelchair, arachnoid metal legs crept over Mr. Uriah's scalp and injected something into his brow, which seemed to relax and sag afterward.

"There are some things about these times, my dear Saul, that make me grateful. Of those things, I believe pain medication is my favorite. Please, join me." Mr. Uriah motioned his hand toward the seat closest to him.

Saul joined him and edged the seat back a few inches. He looked at the old man and tried to recall whether or not his appearance had changed but had difficulty recalling his face at all. In fact, when he thought back to the night they had met, he could recall every detail about the room, about his apparel, mannerisms, and voice, but the face was just a blur.

"You look surprised to see me."

"I'm not sure I know you."

"Of course you know me, Saul. Why else would you be here? I sent for you. Although, I must admit, you did arrive a bit earlier than I had anticipated."

"Be that as it may, I can't place you outside of that chair."

"Yes," Mr. Uriah said before interrupting himself with a dry laugh. "No one sees me outside of this chair."

Above, the retractable ceiling began to close. Somewhere in the room mechanical arms squeaked and whined. If there was someone in the room with them cranking the take up wheel, Saul couldn't see them. He moved toward the edge of his chair.

"You want something from me."

"Not altogether, Saul. It's not that I want anything from you that you, yourself wouldn't want."

A hand appeared from Saul's periphery, startling him. A clean liquid shimmered in a crystal glass.

"I believe gin will suit you better than that swill they served you at Smathers.'"

Saul took the glass and sniffed it. A memory began to surface. Moving evergreens and crisp air.

"Go on. I believe you'll like it a great deal."

Saul tried the drink and found that he did enjoy its dryness and subtle flavor. How was it, he wondered, that Mr. Uriah knew so much about him? Saul eased back into his seat and looked Mr. Uriah in the eyes. Wide and bloodshot, they sat deep in his skull like hidden fruits. The old man gave a toothy grin and pushed a button on his armrest. Again, a mechanical arachnoid rose from the chair, crawled over his scalp, and injected one of its spindly legs into his head.

"I see you're interested in my chair."

"If you're in the mind to tell me, I won't object," Saul said before sipping his gin.

"When I was your age, Saul, I was a vigorous and handsome man. I spent my days as the key fundraiser for the Council of the New Mystical Body and my nights praying and spreading our message to people, specifically people of importance— politicians, city leaders, the wealthiest in the city. The church had a single principle: God is infallible. I was a believer like the church elders had never seen before. I put the Lord before myself at all times. Saul, I could feel the Lord inside me. Not just coursing through my veins, but it was as if He was as much a part of me as my lungs, my kidneys, my—" Uriah's face, which had begun morphing into a glassy emphatic joy, went slack, and shadows once again found refuge in its pits. "My brain. Some days I fell, convulsed with His spirit, spoke in tongues. My brothers saw me as a prophet. The Lord spoke through me. My mind was both human and Lord. The church listened to me and I directed them, for the glory of God. That was until I finally collapsed into a coma. The doctors discovered a large tumor in my brain. My family, who was not sympathetic to my cause, authorized its removal."

Mr. Uriah took a breath and pulled his chair closer to Saul.

"I awoke a changed man. I no longer felt the Lord inside me. I was abandoned by Him. The doctors said the tumor caused my visions."

"I take it you didn't agree with them."

"I felt God inside me, Saul. As much as I can feel my own

hands, I felt Him. And then nothing. There is little difference to me. Whether I was a tool at His hand or I was delusional, there was no cause to make me suffer through that loss. God is a cruel master, wouldn't you agree?"

For no reason for which he could evidence, Saul answered, "No god masters me."

"And this is all the more reason I know that we have found our man." Mr. Uriah paused, as if seeing a memory play out before him. He sighed and said, "As for the chair, it is something I had developed for me. A system of air compressors, wires, and metal. Its legs make it look a bit sinister, but I assure you, it is truly a blissful machine."

30

MR. ERELIM had told David to stand outside a cafe called The Wilted Tulip until a woman with vacant eyes left. He should follow her and report everything she does within twenty-four hours. What exactly Mr. Erelim had meant by vacant eyes, David was unsure, but guessed that he would understand when he saw her, the way that he knew what a glass was when he saw it.

The patrons that came out of the cafe wanted for little. They stepped out with their evening attire and suits and made their way to see plays, go shopping, and visit museums. All of them seemed vacant, but their eyes were perfectly normal.

Mr. Erelim had given him a gun. Inside his pocket, David's finger traced the grooves in the blue steel. It had grown warm against his body. The puzzle of clouds revealed stars and eventually a moon, which cast light between the branches above him. Leaning against a brick fence post, he lowered the brim of his hat so that his face was hidden in shadow.

There was little for him to do but wait. His thoughts centered on the word *vacant*; he thought of how it must feel inside a person's mouth. To say, vacant. Then, as if from some other man's mind, he began to think of how it was possible that he could hear the words he could not speak. His tongue moved inside of his mouth the way he imagined it would when speaking. A warm breeze gathered a discarded newspaper and swirled it a good foot over the sidewalk before letting it fall. There is nothing before this, he thought, only this and nothing before.

Against his better judgment, he closed his eyes and tried to recall his life before waking up in the hotel. He saw black and a small trembling light. Nothing, he thought.

A man approached David.

"Got a smoke for a bum whose down on his luck, mister?"

David shook his head and looked back toward the hotel.

"You don't got to be like that, mister."

A woman walked out of The Wilted Tulip and spoke with the host.

"Mister, I don't suppose you got a dime?"

David felt a hand on his shoulder. Slipping his gun from his pocket, he turned and clubbed the man on the bridge of his nose. The stranger cupped his hands over his face and stumbled back into the shadows of the city park. He opened his mouth as if to speak, but David followed him into the vermilion walkway and clubbed again and again until the man's body lay sprawled in a tangled mess of limbs.

When David walked back to the street, he saw a woman hailing a cab. He'd need to find somewhere more peaceful to observe. David slipped across the street and made his way to an off duty cab sitting behind a large moving truck. He tapped on the window, which the cabbie rolled down.

"Ain't working, mister."

David reached inside the cab, placed his thumbs over the man's eyes, and pressed. There was some resistance but soon he felt the orbs give way to the pressure and shortly thereafter, the body quit shaking altogether.

18

MR. URIAH removed a handgun from a cherry wood box. He slid it across the table as best he could and Saul pulled it into his hands. The weight of it felt right.

"What's to stop me from putting a bullet in you and leaving?"

Mr. Uriah leaned back into his wheelchair and drew a raspy breath through his throat. It hitched there briefly and then crept out. "It's not in you. You will pull the trigger only when you need to."

In the darkness behind the old man, Saul thought he saw a figure stirring. His eyes reflexively moved about their slits. "Are we alone?" he asked.

"Yes. Quite."

"Where are all the people?"

"Which people?"

"The ones who were here earlier."

"They've gone."

"To light the world?"

"You must find our ways peculiar."

"I don't take to people putting words in my mouth."

Mr. Uriah smiled, or Saul thought, had attempted to smile,

but his muscles had lost their full body and so his upper lip rose above his white teeth like a growling dog.

"You have regained your pluck, Saul. This is good. You were rather passive the last time we met."

Saul stood, easing the piece inside his waistband, and said, "If there's nothing else, I need to be on my way."

"And where will you be going?"

Saul hadn't thought about it. His body had wanted to stand and so he did. It was all a bit pointless, he thought, the conversations cloaked in mystery.

"Tell me then, where am I to go? That's what you're getting at, isn't it?"

Mr. Uriah put a finger against his temple, closed his eyes as if reading Saul's mind. It wasn't so, but Saul thought he'd seen the old man's finger dip inside his temple, the first knuckle vanishing completely. Or was it? The dim room made anything uncertain.

"You will wander, my boy. Wander aimlessly until he finds you."

"Who?"

"In good time."

Saul withdrew his piece again. Held it with his finger nearly depressing the trigger.

"Listen, I don't have time for riddles. Who the fuck is gunning for me?"

Mr. Uriah gargled a hollow laugh, a minor chord from an organ of slit throats. It clanked inside Saul's bones, made his stomach soft to hear it. He clipped a shot into the dark, a breath away from Mr. Uriah's ear. The old man held his laugh and curled his lips in agreement.

"Excellent, Saul, that's the spirit. Names I can't give you, for I don't know them, but you'll know to fire when you see yourself."

"Aren't you a damn prophet, then?"

Saul put the gun back in his belt line and left the room though he had good mind to put a shot in the geezer's chest. The way the revolver slipped from his waist, the grace of it, the undeniable equilibrium, was a thing of beauty and this beauty tempted him to bring violence, but just when he had it in his mind to turn and walk back into the large solarium, something held him. A movement in the shadows. Down the corridor. He backed against the concavities of the wall. Edging forward, he saw that there was definitely another man standing by the elevator. The man aped his advance. Saul squinted against the murk and found the man's head moving forward slightly. He moved closer still. The man could, after all, simply be making his way through the darkness as awkwardly as had Saul. There was no immediate threat, Saul assured himself. He stepped from the shadows, as did the man. Saul could see the other's face, the look of death in his eyes.

When he saw the gun, he lifted his hand and fired.

The kick of the gun felt even better this time. However, the man didn't fall. Saul fired three times, but still the body didn't collapse. Time took on a new dimension, quickly gaining depth, and as it began to stretch into that endless space, beginning to collapse under its own weight, the stranger fell apart in pieces. First, his arm; then, his head; finally, his legs.

The hall filled with light.

"Well done, Saul. You've killed yourself."

Saul turned on the lip of his heel to find a blond woman standing in the doorway. Smoke from a long cigarette slithered toward the ceiling. Saul returned his sights to the stranger to find the remains of a full-length mirror scattered at the foot of the elevator.

"You'll learn not to take Mr. Uriah so literally." She traipsed down to him and handed him an envelope. As he pocketed it, she smiled and returned to the suite, closing the door behind her.

THE NIGHT sky had buckled to the relentless advances of the moon; a dusting of light coated the city. Saul navigated through the streets and made his way back to Hotel South where he slinked past the old man at the concierge desk and made his way to room 713. The key didn't turn at first, but after a shimmy, it eased over into its chamber and he stepped inside.

The room had been overturned. In the moonlight, he saw that the couch cushions had been cut, their guts strewn upon the floor. Leaving the lights off, he slipped inside and felt his way through the maze of uprooted furniture until he was snug against the abutment of the two walls. In the veil of black, his ears seemed to expand, collect more sounds than with the lights ignited. Noises of water running within the walls of the building, a fan in a neighboring room, a faucet dripping in the bathroom, the cool hum of a toilet's tank, a car below somewhere backfiring. No steps or breaths or human movement. He was alone with the shadows and a block of pale moonlight resting atop an empty cushion.

The bedroom was in no better shape. Saul made his way along the edges of the hallway, but stopped in the entryway when his foot touched the edge of the mattress. The soft entrails of the bed formed themselves from the gloom, clouds fallen upon the ground to dissolve. Stepping softly, he balanced his weight on the springs of the torn bed. When he was sure that he was alone, he found the overturned lamp and switched it on. With the light upon the ground, the tilted furniture cast strange shadows on the walls, elongated Germanic movie backdrops from an era long since passed.

There was little to find among the mess. Saul picked through drawers, sheets, torn pillows, piles of feathers and cotton, and just as he was about to abandon the search, something caught his attention, a thin sliver of brushed metal glinting beneath the bed frame.

30

THE DELIVERY truck pulled away, a plume of exhaust exploding from its pipe. Although David had rigged a mirror to see people leaving the cafe, he couldn't shake the feeling that he might have missed his mark. He looked into the back seat, the cabby's body crumpled upon the floor, the left leg just above the seat's edge. His cowboy boot pressing against the cushion. They were fine boots.

David turned back to find a thin woman carrying a package in the crook of her elbow hailing a cab. As she stepped into the car, she looked up just long enough to expose her eyes. Vacant. David turned the ignition and began to follow at a distance. Always a car back, David observed the mark through the window of the small sports car before him, the taillights shimmering coals through the beveled glass. Days without sleep loosened his focus, allowed him to drift, if only in part, to some waking dream of a snake fixing on him. The air in the cab became altogether softer and he felt himself being lulled deeper into sleep but stopped himself just shy of resting his eyelids. The cab turned right. He allowed them ample time to make their way along this new street before following.

It was not long, two miles perhaps, of navigating the knotted streets before the cab pulled over and the woman stepped out. She crossed the street and boarded a bus going in the opposite direction. Traffic locked David in his spot. Undeterred, he made a turnabout and followed. By the time he was half the way there, he saw the bus at a stop. Something had gone wrong. The tire flat. The woman with vacant eyes was walking along the boundary of the city park. She stepped between two trees and was gone.

IT BEGAN to rain as he entered the forested park. Although he couldn't remember its name or any landmarks it may have contained, his body guided him with the comfort of having walked through it before. This was the way it was with most of the city. Things appeared to him for what he believed was the first time and his muscle memory took over. This, he believed, was the work of God, the divine hand reaching through the mattress of clouds to aid him in the journey, to protect him and give him strength and wisdom that his mind was not yet capable of processing. In the wood, a city fox scurried among the scrub. The fur, wetted but fiery still in the dim light, was slick against her back. Just before crawling beneath a felled tree, she turned to David and revealed a dead rabbit hanging from her teeth, the rabbit's body limp and heavy. There was a floor of ivy hiding bugs and snakes covering much of the western bank of woodland; David could feel the thicker vines through his soles. The tearing downpour worked to his advantage as it camouflaged the sound of his pursuit. Moisture crept between the edges of his shoes as he stepped through mud and over fallen branches. The woman was wearing unforgiving pumps so David hoped she had removed them and was moving slow enough for him to catch up. Mr. Erelim was right when he'd said that the ways of women were that of deception; that it had been so since she was born of Adam's rib. This woman was no novice. She was a deceiver.

In the distance, David spied the pale flesh of her legs. By the time she reached the edge of the park, he was close enough to see her face. From several yards away, David watched her emerge onto the street, her red leather shoes dangling from her fingers. She walked down a street, and a half block in, she entered a building with a wrought iron gate. David sat in cover. There was something too easy about it. Another ten minutes later, she emerged and snuck into a building across the street. David waited a while longer and then went to the building.

The foyer was unlit. Removing his shoes, he followed the faint wet footprints on the marble floors. The trail barely caught the outside light, but if he angled his head down and to the right, he could just make them out. He tracked until he came upon a long, unlit hallway. A third of the way down, a thin slice of light emerged from beneath a door. There was the sound of a woman humming and the click of a lighter. He took note of the address and returned to his stolen taxicab.

23

THERE WAS little left to do. Shiver and work on his maps. David grabbed a few rags from his flour sack, a handkerchief, a bit of torn dress, and a tie he'd found discarded behind a dancehall. He tucked them inside his coat. From his pocket, he removed a roll of paper and expanded it upon the ground before him. The language, although certainly written in his script, was foreign to him. He touched his fingertip against the jumbled letters. ANMSE LMMMA. What had he been writing? Non-words. At the bottom right corner, were two words he could read: *left shoe.* He briefly thought about this. Looking beyond the bend of his knee, he examined his left shoe, a battered and holey wing tip he'd found behind a shop uptown. David slipped his blackened foot from the leather, and sticking out of the sole's lining, was an edge of paper. After several attempts at fingering it out, he finally managed to remove it and found a key to his map. It took several minutes to remember, but when it came to him, David meticulously began replacing each consonant on the map with a letter seven before it. Vowels required a second decoding, seven letters before and then adding the numerical order in which that letter occurred, minus three.

Hotel South was the first word he was able to decode. A small box at the top left of the map. This square had the number one drawn to the right of it. Following that was Smathers' Bar. "This," he said to himself, "I'm here."

A wind picked up, a howl. In that timbre came the voices once again. There was, as it seemed there always was at such times, a slight tickle at his flesh, something he'd at first found enjoyable, like the fingertips of a lovely woman, combing softly upon him. However, it took, as he knew it would, a turn and those tickles became points of pressure, pushing first in and soon after, outward toward the world beyond. "Don't look," he whispered. "Don't look." The saliva in his mouth grew thick, nearly chewable. They were in his stomach, inching up the walls of his throat, crawling to free themselves. His body became weightless. His mouth began to salivate once more, and then, the vomit. He could feel the grubs mixed with his bile, wringing themselves into crescents upon his lip. At his feet a pile of them, weaving themselves into a foul tapestry. He looked away. Clawed at his skin to remove them. "You're not real," he said. "You're not real." He looked again, but they hadn't left.

A set of feet shuffled behind him in the darkness.

"David, come to me and I can make all of these hallucinations stop."

Even in the gloom, he could see the inhumanly luminous white hair of the man who sought to do him harm.

"No, you'll do to me what you've done to the others."

"He forgives, David. You of all people should know that. He has a great love for you. Your breaks in hallucinations are his act. His kindness."

"No. They're not his doing. They are my doing," David said as he righted himself. He inched into the streetlight.

"Please don't run. I promise you no harm."

The pale light fell on David and he began running. He darted along the sidewalk until his legs felt flimsy and farther still until his pulse deafened him to the world, and yet farther until he was blinded by the light of his body's own desperation. Once the man with the silver hair was no longer in sight, David stepped into an alley and slipped the rack of his ribs between a wall and a dumpster, pushing harder until his entire body had found solace in the shadows. He began tearing his map into small fragments. He would have to remember it.

18

SAUL CRESTED out over the darkling blades of grass in the park and made for a bar he'd seen on his way to the Overbee Hotel. He'd no plan, no idea of what he was to do, just that he was to find a man who looked like him. Upon finding the man, he'd know what to do. He turned the words in his thoughts. With each, he saw an image or function. All except for himself. He could not bring himself to mind. He could bring to memory his shirt, his trousers, the curve of his scalp with the hair slick upon it, but his face was nothing more than a fleshy abstract. This, he assumed, was natural. What man didn't have complications in recalling himself? After all, didn't men spend most of their days staring outside of themselves at others and very little time looking at their own reflections? The very thought of this troubled Saul. The idea of seeing himself in reverse and never naturally. How could a man possibly remember his own face if it was always in reverse?

And so he continued to think upon this until he found himself on a street corner and a new question occupied him: How did he know to cut through the park? This was, as most things were at the time, a question he would table. He made his way into the bar, which he found more comforting than the isolation of Smathers'. He snaked between patrons and bellied up.

A young man with shaved blond hair approached him and raised his eyebrows.

"I'd like a drink. Your choice."

"Sure thing," the man said and collected several other orders.

Saul slipped his finger beneath the seal of the envelop in his pocket and inched it open and took catalog: money, a key, a note. The smell of perfume. The scent of Merav.

Dearest Saul,

Mr. Uriah has asked me to give you these provisions. You will find that there is more than enough money here to last you several weeks. The key is mine. Take a taxi to the following address and let yourself in. I will be waiting for you. As always, destroy this after reading.

331 North Street

Yours,

Merav

He slipped a bill from the stack and handed it to the barkeep, who turned it over a coupled times before handing it back.

"Can't break that. You need something smaller."

"Break it or give me the drink, it doesn't matter much to me," Saul said, taking a deliberate sip from the glass.

The blond made to argue, stopped short, and said, "I'll be back." He walked around the bar and into an office just left of the bathroom.

Tearing the note into pieces Saul tried the clear drink which had the distinct taste of summer plums. It was much softer than the drink he'd had at the last bar and Saul liked this. Yes, he thought, I can't be David.

When the blond came out, he had a stack of bills. He dropped them before Saul and said, "My manager ain't happy."

Saul said, "Perhaps he'd like to come here and register this complaint with me directly."

The blond looked at him like he wanted to say something, but Saul said, "Now fuck off," and the man did.

A man in a collarino and neckband sat next to Saul and signaled to the blond. The bartender brought him a beer and said, "Here you go, Father Tentorio."

Saul pulled the card from his pocket, let it catch the light and spread it in a gradient across the metal.

The priest turned and asked, "Where'd you get that, son?"

Saul said, "I'm no kin to you, Father."

"Yet you still call me Father."

Saul held the card up.

The aging priest pulled it from his fingers and examined it. "It's a most interesting image. A contemporary take on something I've not seen in years. How did you say you came across it?"

"I didn't."

The priest rubbed his fingers over the arms of the angel. He smiled and said, "A man's privacy is his right, I suppose."

"Something like that."

"Do you know who this is? The angel on the card?"

"Do I look like a church man to you?"

The priest took another sip from his beer and said, "How

Tulsa City-County Library
Martin Regional Library

Customer ID: **********8808

Items that you checked out

Title: Light boxes / Shane Jones.
ID: 32345045973899
Due: 2/8/2018 12:00 AM

Title: Mystic river / Dennis Lehane.
ID: 32345082139040
Due: 2/8/2018 12:00 AM

Title:
Shoot like a girl : one woman's dramatic
fight in Afghanistan and on the home
front / Mary Jennings
ID: 32345082156309
Due: 2/8/2018 12:00 AM

Title: The city awake / Dun B. Barlow.
ID: 32345082134645
Due: 2/8/2018 12:00 AM

Title: The drop / Dennis Lehane.
ID: 32345048372008
Due: 2/8/2018 12:00 AM

Total items: 5
Account balance: $0.00
1/25/2018 6:26 PM
Checked out: 14

To renew:
www.tulsalibrary.org
918-549-7323

about this: I'll tell you what I know about this angel and if you feel it's worth something, you can tell me where you found it."

Saul sized up the priest and said, "Sure. If it's useful, I'll bite."

"This angel isn't recognized by the church. His name is Rogziel. He's an angel of wrath. Part of the Apocrypha."

The remnants of Saul's drink seemed to evaporate before his eyes. He shook the glass, letting the alcohol swirl. When the priest saw that his information wasn't enough, he continued.

"This particular card is a calling card from a heretical group of Catholics, who seceded from the Catholic Church in the Middle Ages. They believed that there were parts of the Bible removed for the sake of securing Papal power. Most of the parts they included in their Holy Book were sections about the Virgin Mary, but there are a few sections, very dark sections that dealt with missing years of Jesus Christ, and about the more, let's say, *aggressive* angels. The Catholic Church wanted nothing to do with these radicals and their ideology, so they moved quickly to excommunicate anyone involved."

"They feared a coup?"

"No, worse. They feared the violent and wrathful ideology of those priests."

Saul laughed and threw a glance at the old man sitting next to him.

"You find that amusing?"

"The Catholic Church isn't known for its kind God."

"This should tell you something then, shouldn't it? Even a faction this small, I mean a couple of dozen supporters at best, caused the Papacy to act swiftly. To be honest, I thought they were a thing of the past." The priest turned the card over in his fingers once more and then said, "But this card is too modern."

"So, it's a cult member who left this."

"One of two things: either someone did a bit of research and is attempting to operate under the guise of the old faction, or the faction has managed to survive underground for all these years. I don't know which would be worse."

Saul ordered another drink. The priest slipped the card back and stared at him for a few seconds. Saul felt the old man's eyes on him, crawling across his pores, looking for a way to get inside his head. He refused to look up until the barkeep brought the drink.

"Your turn, son," the priest said after taking a sip of his beer.

"I found it in an overturned room."

"You police?"

"No."

"Then what?"

"Why's a priest out drinking this late anyway?"

The man in the collar laughed and said, "I wander along and see if I can't coax a confession out of some poor soul."

Saul cracked a smile. "I'm a man with a mission he has yet to understand, Father. But even more important," Saul said before he pounded his drink, "late to meet a beautiful woman." He gave a goodbye, a salute of sorts, and stepped onto the street to hail a cab. Just before he got into one, the priest emerged from the bar and said, "Stranger, if you come to understand your mission any better, you can find me down the street at the cathedral."

Saul agreed and stepped into the cab.

30

STRANDS OF MR. Erelim's hair seemed to snake around each other within the nest of white. He made a sudden movement, and without thought, David had his gun pointed. Mr. Erelim didn't move, look away, show concern, only worked at his drink.

"Your intuition is pleasing. However, you shouldn't point your gun at a man who can undo you in less time than it takes to pull your trigger. You may be God's assassin, but I'm God's right hand. You'd do well to remember that, son."

David nodded, still buzzing inside from the urge to fire his piece. To watch the blood blossom behind the old man's head. The metallic smell of it filling the room. David eased the gun back onto his lap and listened.

"Did you turn over the room?"

Nod.

"Did you find anything there? Any addresses?"

Shake.

"Did you leave the card behind?"

Nod.

"Did you make it look accidental?"

Nod.

"Good, we wouldn't want him to feel like he's being gaslit. Curiosity will lead him. You may go now, David. Try to sleep."

David stood and turned toward the fire escape when Mr. Erelim said, "And David, he'll start coming into *his* own now. You're to do away with anyone who might compromise the operation. Even if it's another David."

David drew a long breath in through his nose and made his way out of the window before he'd finished exhaling. He returned to the hotel and sat in the living room, fighting the urge to sleep, his body growing heavy. Finally, he forced himself back to Smathers'. The barkeep brought him a drink. David examined it.

"You ain't thirsty?"

David raised his index finger to his lips, made a silent *shush*.

"Shit on it," the bartender said and walked away.

He would have to sleep at some point. He would have to return to those dreams of shots and carving and silent screaming.

23

THE WIND had turned to whispers again. They found his ears.
Crept in. Laid their eggs. Rolled into the folds of his brain. He
felt them there, hatching. His thoughts would no longer be
his own.

David pulled a pen from his pocket. With a lighter, he
warmed the metal tip until it grew an angry yellow and then
pushed it into his right ear. A pinch of pain ran down his neck
and the stench of burning flesh consumed him. At first there
was a mid-range hum then the ear began to throb, a deep rush
of pain that muted the world with the sound of his own blood.
A man stepped into the alley carrying a large bag. He grew so
close that David was sure he'd hear the angry pulse of his wound.
Pushing his palm against the ear, he crushed the lesion until his
vision went white. The man hefted the bag into the dumpster
and left. As his hearing slowly returned, David listened. There
was only wind. Allowing the relief to take him, he swallowed
hard and rested against the wall, wondering how the old man
found him. Admittedly, he'd spent quite a bit of time scoping
out the bar, but he'd always taken good care to cover himself,
to stay behind the dumpster. David released his ear, steadied
his breath. Maggots would surely come. They would fill his

ear, creep into his lungs, devour him from the inside. He had little time left.

The wind began to rustle the trash around him, catching in a rasp between the bricks and dumpster. *Come, David, come home. We need you, David.* Over and over again until he could no longer bear it and smashed his fist against the wound until he grew dizzy and finally blacked out for a few moments.

He dreamt he was strapped to a table, a doctor checking his vitals. David attempted to speak, but found no language. The doctor held up a syringe. It was filled with violet liquid. The man tapped his finger against the cylinder, the liquid transformed into a colicine of purple maggots. When he tapped once more, they turned into fruit flies, which burst into flight, save for one albino that crawled over David's arm, where it burrowed into the basilic vein and laid eggs.

WHEN HE came to, the sunlight rested upon his chest, hot and angular. David adjusted to the brightness. He saw his intestines unfurled before him like velvet ropes. He scrapped them together, trying desperately to push them back into his body. The wound had sealed. He would need a knife. He would need to cut himself open and place them back inside. As he stood, the sun shifted and caught the sleek ropes upon the ground to reveal that they were not his intestines but foam plumbing wraps. He wondered, had there ever been a time when the world didn't deceive him?

Waves of people flooded the streets, taking with them strollers, bikes, cars, and leaving in the gutters newspapers, cigarettes, and gum. David moved between the currents and navigated to the city square. There, he came across a scratched fountain pen wedged between bricks on a throughway. He proffered from his pocket a scrap of paper and tested the quill. When at first the nib refused to produce, he dolorously released his hands to his side. Thinking to warm the tip, he tried again to much better results.

Customers and tourists ignored him as they spent their time enjoying the warmth of the fine sunny day. David searched for a vantage point where he could observe without being apprehended for being an unsightly supplicant. Even in his worst moments, when the voices shouted and his flesh looked to fall asunder, he knew better than remain in the public. The world did not look kindly on men who had soured and grown thinworn.

Resting against a small waste container, David found several discarded sheets of drywall. Arranging the pieces, he crawled beneath the hypotenuse. A pall of gray dust obscured his vision for a few seconds, but soon his view of the square returned.

18

THE STEPS to Merav's building were finely rounded marble. Despite the years of wear, the surface reflected the light from the moon, which punched through the sky, hot and small. Saul counted the steps as he ascended.

He slid the key into the lock, but Merav opened the door before he could turn it. She reached out and pulled him inside. Saul wasn't sure why, but he nearly asked if Merav was home.

She leaned in, her mouth close enough to his that he could feel its heat. She kissed him softly and asked, "Were you followed?"

"No."

Her lips parted over her teeth in a strange and secretive smile. He'd not seen a smile quite like hers, but when he thought about it, he couldn't remember many smiles. Remnants of Merav's plum lipstick lingered upon Saul's lips. Pressing them together, he pulled them into his mouth to see if they tasted as appetizing as they looked. He was disappointed by the results.

Merav took his hand and led Saul to the bedroom.

THE SUN climbed over the city and crashed into Merav's bedroom. Saul awoke in a sweat. His breath hooked in his throat. He'd had a dream. He was surrounded by words. They stuck to him. His hands at first. Then his chest. The more he struggled to control them, the faster they came. Relentless. Then the world fell all white and cold like some dreadful light and from that light emerged a room of beds thinly veiled by hospital curtains. He was buckled down, his veins crawling from him and connecting to machines. Violet blood pulsing inside the thin membrane. In the distance, he heard a German man speaking but he could not decipher his words outside of a number: *achtzehn*.

He sat up in a mess of sheets and began to untangle himself. Staring at the sharp angle of the sun along the wall, he worked through the dream. Eighteen. How was it that he knew German? Had he been in the war? Was his memory loss a battle trauma? Saul stood and searched for his clothes. There was a terrible silence in the apartment. Walking heavily, he attempted to assuage the isolation, but found the sound of his feet upon the wood too haunting. Under the bed, in a tidy stack, were his folded clothes, the gun, and a note resting on a box.

A foolish man falls asleep in bed with a stranger. A dead man sleeps without his gun. Enjoy the gift. – Merav

Saul dressed. He opened the box to find an expensive suit coat folded inside red tissue paper. The cloth was identical to his trousers. Sliding the cool silk lining over his arms, Saul pulled the jacket to and examined himself in the mirror. It was a perfect fit. A match with the clothing he woke in.

He checked the gun's chamber. He couldn't shake the idea that he was being played. It was time for him to chase down his first clue.

UNION STATION. The vaulted ceilings and stained glass made the place look like a church. In the rafters, birds darted between beams, their calls lost in the sound of foot traffic. People rushed down stairs, through halls, into shops. Some stood, confused. A slow motion plane among the living, Saul kept his own pace, forcing the throng of travelers to flow around him.

Along the corridor were murals of the city, a city the artist had imagined during a period of war. Men in gas masks holding angels with mechanical arms. The winged creatures reaching toward the heavens but unable to flee the soldiers' grip. A strange sense of weightlessness overtook Saul and he found himself smiling.

When he approached the lockers in the west annex of the station, the number of boxes overwhelmed him. Thousands of locked metal doors. The walls seemed to inch in as Saul looked for numbers. How, he wondered, did anyone get into the lockers at the top? Reaching his hand as far as he could, it was only possible to touch the bottom of the second to last row of security boxes.

He located locker 316 and automatically entered a combination, 0523. Was this similar to the words he saw, some innate function of his mind that seemed to operate of its own accord? When the door clicked open, Saul pulled it wide to reveal a worn photograph.

The man in the photo was fair-haired, eyes to match. He brooded at the camera, the look of a killer. Creases along his forehead looked to be cut by a heavy hand. Saul flipped the photo over to find written directions: *face a mirror and hold this photo before you.* He slipped it into his pocket and made his way to a restroom. Without pause, the tide of commuters streamed around him, all dressed for work, suitcases in their hands. Saul walked against the current.

Upon finding the men's room, Saul escaped the chaos to find the bathroom deserted save for an old janitor shuffling in the corner, sweeping at some invisible pile. Saul stood before a mirror and held the photo. The muscles in his jaw tightened and slackened and the photo began to tremble in his hand.

Saul leaned over the sink and inspected himself. He ran his fingers along the ridge of his jaw. Then ran them through his hair. As they parted, he saw something on his scalp. Leaning closer to the mirror, he spread the hair with his fingertips and saw, for the first time above his ear, a small eighteen tattooed beneath the hair.

"It is a very good picture of you," the janitor said, without looking from his duties.

"You'll do well to mind your business," Saul said.

The janitor apologized and fell to his knees to sweep nothing in particular into his hands.

30

DAVID AWOKE to find Mr. Erelim standing in the corner of his room. It was difficult to see him at first, as if he were an abstract embellishment in the wallpaper. The form slowly manifested into the boxy old man he'd met in the bar as David found focus.

The lights came on and the older man said, "We must speak."

The word *speak* bothered David. Was there ever speaking? Had he ever known the language of tongues? He made no sign of understanding. Instead, he looked at Mr. Erelim with narrowed eyes, closing them to feign sleep.

Mr. Erelim clapped his hands together and said, "Listen."

David slicked his hand against his scalp and obliged.

"We are searching for an old man who goes by the name Uriah. Either the woman or the David she's leading around like a dog will guide you to him. We have learned that the woman goes by Merav and the man calls himself Saul. There is no mistaking Uriah. He's in a wheelchair. A sickly old mess. You have permission to kill him on sight."

David nodded.

"There are a few other things. Some loose ends I need to clean up. A few from the Council who have strayed. One roams in the alley. He could be a threat. I will see to him. However,

I want you to be certain you're following the right man. Am I understood?"

David signaled and stood, his clothes less tidy than they had been the night he first awoke. He checked his piece, what light existed in the room spread in a smooth gradient along the barrel. A longing to shoot rose in him. He grimaced and slipped it in his waistband.

Mr. Erelim, upon reading David's expression, said, "If the woman or man gives you any trouble, you can take care of them after you deal with the old man."

Mr. Erelim exited the apartment and David followed him. They walked past the old concierge at the counter and into the street. The sun floated between buildings, a dull peach globe in a bath of smog. Without a word, the old man vanished into the foot traffic as if he'd stepped off the edge of the earth. David navigated through the streams of people until he turned down an alley and saw a young man loading a suitcase into a black luxury sedan.

As David approached, the man turned around, scowled, and reached for a tire iron, but his effort was for naught as David had laid hands upon his neck before his feet could find purchase on the smooth cement.

The break was unsatisfying. A twist, a dull pop, and a release of breath, a whisper, a last word. Perhaps *no*. David removed the suitcase and folded the body into the trunk.

The sedan drove much smoother than the taxi. David gripped the mahogany steering wheel. He thought of bending it, of its healthy snap. He continued to hold the wheel as he sat in front of the woman's apartment. A pair of lovers snuck into a door well and began to kiss, the man reaching his hand up the thigh and below the skirt. Nothing stirred inside of David. He continued to watch, aware of his detachment. This, he thought, was to be human. There came from within him a motivation to twist the wood beneath his hands, which he did.

MERAV ARRIVED at her apartment, making the usual detour. After several moments, a window grew full with light. Tiring of the sedan, David chose to investigate. Each landing in the stairwell provided a good opportunity for an attack, a feature that was currently beneficial to him, but one that could prove to be problematic in the future. He leaned with his back against the wall and committed to memory the natural splay of shadows.

He began to fixate on the word *shadow*. He examined it in his head, thought of each letter projecting a shadow onto the earth, each letter a marbleized tribute to man. Still, he moved his tongue inside his mouth, rubbing it against the ridges of his teeth. Several floors below he heard a door open, a man speak, and a woman walk onto the street. David descended the steps, his shoes hissing against the stone.

When he returned to the car, two patrol cops were strolling down the sidewalk discussing the big fight they'd recently heard on the radio. One of the men made to say something to David. As he opened his mouth, David fingered the gun in his pocket.

The smaller officer tugged on the cuff of the former and said, "Kelly, it's time to head back, shift's over."

Kelly smiled and said, "Let's go."

After the men walked away, David slipped into the car. Disappointment weighed in his belly.

HUNGER PANGS became distracting. David had finished the remainder of his dried meats and figs. Days had passed without so much as a sign. He'd seen a diner a few blocks away. Leaving the car, he moved through the night, avoiding pyramids of light that stood beneath the streetlamps.

Inside the diner, he ordered a burger to go. The cashier went to the back and tacked a sheet of paper to a metal wheel. There was one patron in the diner, an anxious young man who drank coffee and scribbled in a notebook. He looked at David, and when David stared at him unflinching, the young man gazed into his coffee and did not look back up. As the waiter bagged his food, David ordered a blueberry pie on display in a glass cake plate. He took bites out of the burger as he walked back to his car. The meat warmed him. There was nothing in that moment but the grinding of bread, grease, and muscle.

The night weighed against him. Moisture on the leaves reflected the streetlights—a thousand glowing, trembling eyes staring at him. The city was always damp, always shimmering light, always filthy. How the unadulterated sun felt upon his skin, he couldn't remember, but he had the idea that it felt nice, dry. When light did make it through the bank of clouds that clung to the city, it was only briefly. A reminder that the world was not alone, that something greater lay beyond. Something majestic and whole. David allowed the word *whole* to repeat in his thoughts. He felt whole, his mission clear, but when he was in these isolated moments where his hands were tasked with the mundane realities of living, he longed for more.

A shuffling sound emerged from a door well and a hand fell upon his arm. David dropped his meal and had a stranger's hand bent backwards before the man could say a word.

The vagrant, swathed in layers of dingy suit coats, front teeth missing, cried, "I just wanted change. I just wanted change."

David slipped his fingers into the man's mouth, forcing his tongue still. The thin man struggled against him, but could not manage to break away. Considering the problematic logistics of keeping two bodies in the sedan, David released the man.

"Thank you," the drifter said, his voice hoarse. He gathered the cloth satchel, stumbled back a few feet. When it was clear that David wasn't going to pursue him, the man turned and ran.

The hamburger was a loss, but the pie could be salvaged. Scraping handfuls of blueberries and crust into his mouth, David ate until he felt fullness, but not so much as to be gluttonous. He put away the remainder of the pie and continued to keep watch as dawn took the sky with a mist of rain that slicked the roads and blurred his windows.

THE WOMAN was no fool. She walked with confidence, but changed routes often, doubling back sometimes in strange ways, ducking into shops, emerging from different doors. She walked into an indoor market, a labyrinth of Asian fish vendors, shoe shops, bakeries, and curiosity booths. David followed her to a shoe boutique.

The glass ceiling of the market crackled with a heavy rain. A rush of people filled the halls as they escaped the sudden downpour. David entered a store opposite the shoe boutique. A short man with a muff of hair along the sides of his bare head approached him.

"It is strange storm," the man said—his Japanese accent thick, almost too difficult for David to decipher.

David agreed.

"Umbrella?" the man asked, pointing to a bucket of them.

At first David waved him away, but then stopped the clerk and made a motion as if he was putting on a coat.

"Yes. Trench coat."

David then signaled for a hat and the salesman vanished behind a curtain. Across the walkway, Merav slipped into a pair of crimson pumps. She twisted them in the light, examining the seams and heels. Putting a finger on the toe, she spoke to the woman standing above her.

"These should fit," the man said as he handed David a gray trench coat and a fedora.

David slipped them on and found that they did indeed fit. He handed the man some bills. The salesman attempted to give him change, but David moved the small man out of the way when he noticed that the woman had vanished. He took to the hall, and as a horde of shoppers passed around him, he spied a back hallway that snuck around rear of the shoe boutique. Down that back hall, the woman's heels clicked in the distance. However, no matter how swift his pace, he couldn't seem to gain ground on her. The strange tributary was all angles and turns. He kept his finger on the handle of his piece, just in case she should get the jump on him.

David stopped at a fork in the hall. A whisper came to his ear, *She went left.*

Turning around, his gun in hand, he found no one behind him. David stepped left, but something about it didn't feel right to him. Too obvious. He slipped off his shoes. Walked right. Through the exit door, David emerged to find the woman halfway down the street. He re-shoed and blended into traffic.

Though the rain had let up, a steady drizzle slicked his new jacket and hat.

23

WAKE UP. The voice came to David as he teetered on the edge of sleep. *They're coming*, it said. His arm began to itch again. Without looking, he eased his fingers over the crook of it and began to scratch. When no relief came and the urge to dig into his flesh arose, David rubbed his forearm against the rough edge of a drywall slab. Still, the distinct sensation of tiny hooked mouths clearing away his flesh increased. He repeated, "Don't look," as he crawled out of his shelter. He would need to walk around, see if the night air didn't take his mind off it. Dispel the grubs. Quell the voices.

He left the alley and emerged into foot traffic. He made his way to the fountain at the center of town square. There, he saw three women wearing little more than loincloths and swatches of gold fabric across their chests. In a triangle, they stood mesmerized by the playful stream pouring from Pan's Flute. From behind their backs, each woman withdrew three fiery batons. They began to juggle them without a sound. David stood transfixed by their grace. He moved closer, and just as he reached one of the women, they began tossing their batons to the left. The sudden change startled David. He jumped back and covered his face.

A small boy on the fringe of the crowd laughed. The taunt made David's ears hot. One of the jugglers turned and faced him. She handed him one of her batons. He grabbed it. Pulled it closer to his face. His scalp tightened as it puckered into a thousand tiny bumps. He thought to bring it to his clothes. His hand began to move the baton closer, but before it touched his shirt, the juggler snatched it from him.

"These flames bring life, not destroy it," she said, a thick Romanian accent breaking the sentence in odd places. She blew David a small kiss and returned to her sisters. He edged closer, never taking his eyes off the juggling beauty. Her arms pushed and pulled as the rods whirled about.

The tallest of the women spoke, "We will be in Saint's Park for three nights. Bring the family."

The women formed a line and walked away, flames still dancing above their heads. David followed them through the streets until he was in a large field on the edge of the city park. Several large performance tents huddled in the lot. Their fabric torn but crudely stitched together with the aid of various flags. Black trucks, spotted with rust, hummed as their retrofitted generators pulsed life into a web of hanging lights.

David continued to tail the women until one curled her finger and told him to join her. He followed her into a tent at the farthest end of the park. It was dark. As his eyes adjusted, a small orb of amber light birthed under its glow a wheelchair with a pale figure half submerged in shadow.

The woman's voice came from the blackest part of the tent. "Iosif, we have a visitor."

The gray body shifted, its spine pulling the torso from the void of night. Climbing one vertebra at a time, Iosif revealed his sickly body. Thin and slick with sweat, he twisted until finally exposing his head, a swollen thing, which tapered to a point like a spider's abdomen. Iosif gave a deep-throated hiss, a claim to air, and in a child's voice, whispered, "Are you lost?"

"I'm not," David replied.

"Why have you followed?" Iosif shifted in his chair, pulled his fingerless fist into his mouth, sucked.

"I followed this woman."

Iosif released a cough. "Only lost men follow women," he said.

The fire dancer emerged from the gloom, her clothes gone.

"Iosif can tell your fortune, stranger," she said.

David felt his skin loosening about him. The world of flesh coming undone. Folding his arms about his chest, he shook his head.

"Ileana," whispered the man-child. "Bring him closer."

The woman pulled David into her arms. Her breath warm on his neck. She took his hand into hers and led him closer to Iosif.

"Please," Iosif said, "lean closer."

David eased forward. When he had grown too close, he began to pull back, but it was too late. Iosif's spindly arms wrapped around his neck, then a toothless mouth sucked upon his eyebrow. David thrashed against the attack, but soon found the air to grow unbearably thin. His mind floated into the soup of dull light and then all fell dark.

DAVID AWOKE on a bed inside a trailer. The pale sun was high and he was warm for the first time in weeks. He was bathed and smelled of lineament and peppermint oils. Slipping out of bed, he searched for his clothing. The sun poured through a skylight in a column of white. Dry skin floated through the beam and suddenly David felt as if he might be underwater. Wrapping a sheet around his waist, he shuffled across the room, looking for his clothes. The wall opposite him was made up of locking drawers. He fingered the locks apart and spied the contents of several, finding only sheets. When he turned, he found Ileana resting on the bed, her legs crossed, his clothing folded upon her lap.

"You slept for a very long time, David."

The blood in his ears grew hot.

"What have you done to me?"

"I've cleaned you, David."

"I never told you my name."

"Iosif saw your name, David. He saw many things." Ileana stood and handed him his clothes. "We need to talk after you are dressed. I will wait for you in my trailer."

"How will I find it?"

"It's the only one with my sisters and me painted on it." She smiled and left.

The last time his clothing smelled fresh was when he'd awakened in his hotel. At that time his shirt smelled of chemicals. Now they smelled like flowers. His nails were clipped and clean. His wounds treated. The skin on his arms captured the sunlight in a gentle gradient. There was nothing wriggling inside him. No voices calling to him.

When David arrived at the proper trailer, he found Ileana at a table pouring two cups of warm tea.

"You look fetching," she said.

Sniffing his cuff, David said, "It smells like flowers."

"Freesia. The Africans use it to reduce odor."

"You've been to Africa?"

"I've been many places, David. Please, have a seat." Ileana waved toward an empty chair.

David did as she requested and took a sip of the tea.

"Your voices have quieted down."

"How did you know?"

"You appear rested. This helps. But the voices aren't your problem, insomnia is. Isn't it?"

"Yes."

"A soldier who cannot sleep is not an asset."

A pink thread of pain ran through David's temple. "Why did you say that?"

"Iosif saw many things."

The previous night flooded back into David's mind. The fire, the circus, the strange man-child in a rolling chair. "Did he heal me?"

Ileana blew a silent whistle, a seductive breath, and said, "I'm sorry, David, but there is no cure." When she saw David's brow lower, she added, "But, I believe Iosif discovered information that will aid you with your journey."

He sipped his yarrow tea and signaled for her to continue.

"There is a man who looks like you. You and he share dreams. Search for him. He will likely be with a woman with chameleon hair. She sides with a vengeful old man. You must not be seen by the old man, or the woman. Do you understand?"

"Yes, but why?"

"The snake will eat his tail."

"What do you mean?"

"I do not know. This is what he told me. This is all he knows about that. Please, David, that is not the important part. What you must know is that you have to help this man who looks like you. There is something different about him. Some defect, such as you have, that will make his mission very difficult. You must lead him to the truth so that you both may live."

"What?"

"Again, this was not revealed to Iosif." She took a drink of her tea and added, "There is one last thing."

"Yes."

"There are others. Others who look like you. You must not mistake them." Ileana looked down to her teacup. She took a drink and closed her eyes tightly, as if blocking something out.

"There is something you're not telling me. Isn't there?"

She shook her head. "I cannot tell you. It may change your destiny."

"Why did you choose me?"

"I didn't. You chose me. Iosif sends us out when we arrive in a city. Whenever someone follows us, we lead him to Iosif. It is his only way to experience the world. He is trapped inside that—" She paused as if holding back a sob, and then finished, "—that twisted prison. He has such a beautiful mind, David."

Before David could ask another question, a half-sized man opened the door and said, "Man's got to leave, Ileana."

The woman stood and David followed her out of the car. She touched his cheek and whispered, "I'm sorry, but your visions will return very soon."

A weightlifter walked between the two and said, "You follow me and don't come back."

David agreed.

Just before he was out of ear shot, Ileana called out to him, "David, I almost forgot to ask: does the number twenty-three mean anything to you?"

"No."

She blew him a kiss and said, "Goodbye."

18

STEAM CREPT through sewer grates. The vapors snaked through the metal teeth and along the edge of Saul's calves. He stepped onto the street and raised a hand. After several moments, a yellow car pulled up beside him and he climbed inside.

"The Wilted Tulip."

"You got it," the driver said and pulled away. As they swerved between cars and the driver cursed, Saul took out the photograph and examined it. He tried to commit the face memory. The square jawline. The thin eyebrows. The wrinkles along the temples. He'd never thought of his age before. It occurred to him that he'd never thought about many things that others must take for granted. Author of all language, he thought. God's image. He saw the words in his thoughts. Played with them. Switched them around. They were hollow. Changeable. Impermanent. Like man. You kill a man, you kill his language.

"How long you live in the city?"

Saul stared at the man through the rearview. He ignored the question.

The driver asked again.

"I heard you the first time," David said and returned his gaze to the photograph. He closed his eyes and attempted to recall the features of his face. He could only imagine the word *face*. His hand, as if in possession of its own mind, crept to his head and rubbed the number on his scalp. Before too long, the cab arrived at the café and Saul handed the cabbie fare and a handsome gratuity.

He took a table by the sidewalk and ordered a drink. The city was transitioning between the mandatory hours of the workday and the freedom of the weekend. It seemed as though the walking traffic had a bounce to its step, an excitement to drink and dine and dance. He kept a watchful eye, the photograph in his hand. At one point, he saw a slender man with slicked hair and trousers much like his own. However, when Saul compared the photograph to the man's face, there was little else in common.

From the clicking of pedestrian traffic came the familiar whisper of a woman. *Don't be so obvious.*

He slid the photo into his pocket and surveyed the patio. The waiter returned with his drink. As Saul reached for cash, the man said, "No need, sir. Compliments of the woman over there."

A woman with curly brown hair and a powder blue dress sat behind him with her back against the wall. She drew a long breath from her cigarette. He'd know that inhale anywhere.

Merav inclined her head, and Saul walked to her table.

"Is that your voice I hear inside my head?"

She turned and looked toward the street. A wounded pigeon pecked at something. She sighed and said, "What did I say about questions?"

Saul's trigger finger clenched at the air. Sipping his drink to allow the urge to subside, he tried to rephrase the question without saying more than he should.

"Tell me why I can hear your voice in my head."

A long drag off her smoke. A look to her fingers. "I'm a biloquist."

"I'm sure in some circles that's a common word." David countered the urge to leave by trying to remember the face in the photograph, his face.

"I can project my voice."

She was cool, dismissive. A few seconds passed when Merav looked to be still, as if sleeping. The daylight spread across the lenses of her sunglasses in a dull gray paste. Saul saw himself in them, the foot traffic streaming behind him, headless and small.

"You have a photograph of something."

"I'm sure it's something you or the old man planted for me."

"I'm not aware of everything Mr. Uriah does."

"The old fruit couldn't have planted this where I found it."

"If you know what's good for you, you'll show him some respect. He's your only ally," Merav said. She took a drag off her cigarette, blew the smoke, and as she did, he found himself frustrated by her distance.

She said, "What makes you so sure he isn't responsible?"

Saul said, "Don't ask questions. It makes you look weak."

A sharp pain burst into Saul's knee. Before he could process its cause, Merav pulled a small penknife from beneath the table, his blood stained the tip.

"If it weren't for Mr. Uriah, I'd have killed you for that."

A wall of silence. Saul built it. Each second a brick. It was all he could do to stop his rising urge to strike her.

"How did you find the photograph?"

"A note in a pack of matches I found in the hotel."

"I'm not Mr. Uriah's only employee, Saul. I'm sure he's responsible. At least, you better pray he was."

"I don't pray."

She thought for some time, her large sunglasses hiding her eyes, making it very difficult for Saul to assess her mood. However, he was sure it wasn't good. The wound in his knee began throbbing. He thought of telling her about the number on his scalp, but opted to keep it to himself.

"It's likely that Mr. Uriah would have told me. Let me see this photograph."

Saul slipped it from his trouser pocket and gave it to her. She smiled as she rubbed the worn edges of the image.

"It's a flattering photo of you, Saul."

"Why was a photo of me in a subway locker?"

"It does concern me. We need to see Mr. Uriah."

Saul finished his drink and watched Merav leave the table. As her hips moved inside her form-fitting dress, his anger melted away. He was reminded of why he'd followed her in the first place. Why he'd let his guard down. Why he'd awakened tired that morning.

MR. URIAH examined the photograph. It trembled in his frail hands. Air wheezed from the opening in his trachea. Merav stood behind him. She rubbed his bony shoulders and watched him examine the photograph as if she might learn something, as if the way he looked at the image was somehow unique. He set it down and stared at a massive painting of a Barron in regalia. There were several large paintings like this along the wall, each three feet apart. Decorations to cover the unsightly window plugs. Saul wondered what would happen if he shot one of the paintings, let sunlight pour atop the old man. Would he turn to ash? Hold his shape for a time before crumbling beneath his own weight?

"This is unfortunate," Mr. Uriah said.

Merav put her hands on Mr. Uriah's head, lightly caressing the patchwork of scars and flesh. The breath of a small air pump came. Merav stepped back as the medicine spider did its job. Mr. Uriah let go a small moan of pleasure and then said, "You have no memory of leaving this note?"

"I have no memory of a damn thing before I woke."

"They are thorough. I can't fault them in that."

"There's also this," Saul said, pulling the silver card from his breast pocket.

A reverse hiss came from Mr. Uriah's throat. He opened his hands wide like a child to candy. "Where did you find this?" he asked, a pause between each word.

"I found it in my overturned apartment."

"That is most disappointing," Mr. Uriah said, reaching for the card. "We'll find you somewhere else to stay. I suppose a good thing couldn't last."

"What does that mean?"

"The discovery."

Saul pulled the card away from the old man's fingers. "I need some answers, Uriah. I'm tired of all the goddamned mystery."

Mr. Uriah set to laughing. Saul slipped the card into his pocket and removed his gun.

Merav stepped in front of the wheelchair. "Saul, don't be a fool."

The old man's ghostly laugh slipped around Merav. He put

his spindly hand on her hip and ushered her out of his view.

"Yes, Saul. You've found your equilibrium. This is good. The card must have been dropped by one of Erelim's henchmen. It's a fortuitous find for us."

"Who is Erelim?"

"One of the Council's men. I've never met him personally. Some of the people who were at my level spoke of him as if he'd been sent by the Lord himself. All manner of stories they'd tell about him."

"What do you mean at your level? I thought you were respected."

Mr. Uriah rolled back, the shadows palming his brow. "Oh, Saul, I was, but that doesn't mean I was a top ranking official. There were levels that none of us had ever seen. Some that those directly above me hadn't seen either. That card gives security clearance into some of the more exclusive offices of the Council. It's a type of key. Oh, what I wouldn't give to see those secured buildings. But as you see, Saul, I'm too fragile to go anywhere."

Saul put his piece away and pulled the card out again. He let the light run over it. Turned it to better see the engraving. "Why didn't you—" Saul began, pausing as he ran his finger tip over the image, "just pay to have someone make a duplicate?"

"I tried. Used some of the best counterfeiters and locksmiths in the city. It's coded, you see. It's more complex than your eye can comprehend, or your touch. Eventually I gave up on the idea. I only knew what it looked like. I'd never touched one, so I could never get an original to give it a proper try." Mr. Uriah touched his thumbnail to his lip and then said, "I'd heard rumor that one man did. He stole the card somehow. They say the Council cut his hand off and sent it to the counterfeiter as a warning. Can you imagine? Receiving a severed hand clutching the card you'd made? It's barbaric."

"Is this true?"

"One can never say, my dear. There are many stories passed between members of the Council. You simply get to the point where you believe what you hear because often the truth is far worse than the stories. However, the story I'm about to tell you is, in fact, true, despite how daft it may seem."

Saul leaned back into his seat. Merav brought him a drink and sat at his side. Mr. Uriah pushed a button on his chair, and as the medicine was injected in his head, he began, "There is a hidden lab in this city."

"I don't get it," Saul said. "What's this all about?"

"There were a group of scientists who were displaced after the war. Some were hired by Russia. Some by the United States. Given amnesty for their contributions to advancing the agendas of sovereign nations. Some, however, were acquired by private parties." He paused to catch his breath. "The Council is trying to create the perfect body. Adam before the fall."

"To what end?"

"Imagine," Uriah said, "a new inquisition, a world of men built for the glory of God. There's no telling the real plan. The Council operates in cells. No one knows who's at the top. Who's giving the orders." He rolled his chair back, looked to the ceiling as if tracing a thought along a fine crack in the plaster. "From what we have ascertained, they plan to seize power of the church first."

"Why should I care? Let them take the church."

"You are in too deep. They are on to you now, Saul." Mr. Uriah's voice was growing weaker. His eyelids tightening.

"You okay?"

"I'm sorry, Saul," Uriah began, his eyelids wavering.

Merav stood up and said, "He needs rest."

There were more questions Saul wanted to ask, but opted to let things be for the time. "Okay. I'll let you see to him. But I'll have more questions."

"I'm sure you will."

23

It took some time, but the voices began to return. David used a bathroom in the bus station. As his urine spider-eyed the toilet water, the bubbles began winking, then talking.

Earl him.

He stared into the bowl. "You're not real."

Listen, came the reply.

"No."

Yes.

"No."

Earl him.

He could hear their voices bounce around the stall. Their reverberation as natural as was his own. David leaned in closer, his neck nearly against the porcelain rim. The bubbles gasped into extinction. When they had gone to waste and the liquid lay flat, he stood up and left the stall. Back in the bus terminal, passengers awaited their departure. It was oddly quiet. Occasionally, a public address speaker came to life for an announcement. A shadow grew along the corridor as the sun sank behind the jagged scalp of the city. Two janitors leaned against a bulletin board. The taller of the two examined his watch and yawned.

A bus rolled into a parking space and a queue of people formed at the gate. The passenger door hissed open and the line inched forward. David had heard of men put on buses by the city, madmen sent with a one-way ticket to other towns. He perched on a bench and thought about the bubbles. Normally the voices were negative. They coaxed him to dig at his flesh, to step in front of cars. The bubbles were different. He turned the words *Earl him* over in his head. Was it code? he wondered, a riddle placed in him by a man-child.

A janitor placed his hand on David's back.

"Sir, you'll need to leave if you ain't waiting on a bus."

BENEATH THE slats of drywall, David lay with his hands stuffed inside his jacket. The night had taken the city and the cold returned to him. Sleep began to take him. The world became soft around the edges, grew distant. He closed his eyes. It was like floating. He envisioned the man with white hair, a halo of bubbles around his head. Then, as usual, David's legs shook and he was alert.

Rolling onto his side, David faced a soup can trod flat, the jagged edges catching the street lights. Earl him. Something came to him then. Perhaps a memory. The man with white hair. His name. Mr. Earlham. But that wasn't it. Something close. David thought back to Ileana. She had said something about an old man. But she said wheelchair. David tried to recall his first meeting with the man with white hair.

They'd had a drink. There was some talk of a mission. God's work. He'd been scratching his arm at the table and the man asked him about his visions. Were they still there? They walked outside and the man tried to put his hands around David's neck. Erelim. It was Erelim who was looking for people like him.

David wormed his way out of the shelter and walked back to Smathers'. Once there, he hid behind the dumpster and kept watch. If the old man returned, he'd follow him.

30

Mr. Erelim sat without a word for a long time. David could feel him searching for honesty. What else was there? David wondered. In his life, there was only truth. It came as his silence.

"Lost her?" Erelim asked. "How did you lose her?"

David removed a piece of paper and wrote: *She went into a marketplace. Foot traffic during a rainstorm.*

Mr. Erelim swam in his ideas, his eyes seeming to trace each around the room.

"Have you seen Saul yet?"

No.

"He's likely returning to himself. Comfortable in his skin. He'll be more difficult to follow. He and you are similar in many ways. However, he has fallen to the habits of the flesh."

David wrote: *I will stay with the woman. He will show.*

"You truly are made in God's image, son."

David left the building and returned to the front of Merav's. There he waited. An undulant fringe of an awning waved in the breeze. A soft clapping. He took up with thoughts of how he might kill the woman. It seemed to him the execution of a woman should be different than that of a man. A male required

91

brute strength, decision, speed. A woman, although crafty in her own right, deserved a much softer death. He could simply snap her neck to spare her the pain of knowing death was upon her. He could choke her, staring into her eyes, making his own eyes soft, as if he were willing her to death and she following his lead. Perhaps he might even slip into her room while she slept and do her in while she was tangled in those delicate affairs of her dreams. Despite all the scenarios he invented, he knew that it would most likely not transpire peacefully. Dealing death rarely went as planned. No, she would most likely fight, kick against his legs with her piercing heels.

He twisted his hands around the steering wheel, wishing he could hear it snap. The rain picked up again and his windshield went awash in blur.

29

He awoke in his bed, fully clothed. In his right pocket, he found a note that read, *You are David. You were made in God's image. You are the author of all language, emender of sins.*

David couldn't remember entering the room. Nothing there seemed to belong to him. A dull ache began to emerge from the back of his head. A barbed sun, rising. Leaning over some, David made his way out of the bed. The slight movement seemed to alleviate the discomfort. Leaving the hotel room, he made his way to the concierge.

"Excuse me, sir."

An old man sitting with his back to the service window turned around reluctantly. He stared at David, the shadows of the room gathering in his eyes.

"Smathers' is down the street."

"Be that as it may, it's not the question I had for you."

The man sat there, his brow furrowed as if he didn't understand the language. He pointed behind him and said, "Smathers' is down the street there."

"How did I get to my room?"

"I'm sorry?"

"I said, how did I get to my room?"

"Same way as always, I guess."

"What does that mean?"

The old man scratched his head and followed, "You got there."

Patience wearing thin, David attempted another approach, "How much do I owe you for the night?"

"You don't pay. The other guy does."

"What other guy?"

"The other guy," the old man said, turning around and looking at his radio. He turned the volume up and said, "Just go to the bar."

David walked to a door at the side of the small greeting station and opened it. The old man, too surprised to move, stared at him as he approached. Slipping his hands around the old man's throat, David said, "The thing about life is that it's easily shucked from a body. People spend their entire lives hurtling toward some moment in time when they are upended. Precious moments all added together for one event in time, and as one reaches that moment, he must suddenly try to recall those countless instances where he squandered away his life with radio, napping, dull jobs, and pointless conversations. He must find himself accountable at that exact time in his life and understand that his life, the seemingly endless collection of days, would soon be out of his control, and it is at this time he must come to an epiphany that if he is to escape this fate that seems to be barreling toward him, he can either change his life and seek some higher purpose, some calling, if you will, or revert to his old habits of lazing about, cutting corners, and breaking rules and potentially, no, certainly finding himself back in this situation again. You have reached such a point, have you not?"

The hotelkeeper spoke through his constricted throat, "Please, mister—"

"Have you not?"

"Yessir."

"Then tell me what I want to know and you can choose to continue to waste your life in front of this radio or escape forever this particular situation in which you find yourself."

The old man agreed and David released him. Rubbing his throat, the old man said, "I don't know shit. All I know is an old guy with white hair pays for all the rooms in this hotel. He instructs me to tell you to go to the bar. I assume he meets you there."

"What's his name?"

"He pays in cash and I don't ask. When there's repairs need made, he pays those fees, too."

David pulled the register pad from the counter. There was nothing written on any of the lines. A fine coat of dust clung to the binding. Watching the old man finger the agitated flesh that hung loosely around his collar bone, David let the pages fall one-by-one.

"If I go to that bar and the man isn't there, I'm coming back. Understood?"

The old man said, "I ain't lying."

"If I do come back and you aren't here, I'll burn this place to ground. Is that understood?"

Again, the old man proclaimed his innocence.

As David left the hotel, the man said, "Tell him I didn't sign up for none of this."

THE NIGHT was warm and the air rubbed his skin in a way that he found generally displeasing. Wiping a line of sweat away from his brow, he thought about the room. He attempted to bring back some memory of having been there. Of an old man with white hair. As he crossed over the bricks of an alley, a small rat darted out toward the street. Its damp fur black as the puddles among the brick. David lifted his foot and brought the lip of his heel down onto the neck of the thing. It gave a faint squeal as his foot pulled the head away from the body, leaving it in spasms. David cleared the gore and found his way to the bar.

Inside was barely lit. A black man played a piano. The high notes crawled inside David's head. He nearly buckled from pain, as if shot through with needles. Stumbling, he grabbed hold of the bar and righted himself as best he could.

"You okay, David?" the bartender asked. "You don't look real good."

"Whiskey."

The barkeep pulled a bottle and served him. David swallowed the drink in a gulp and signaled for more. He did this several more times before the room seemed to grow softer and the noise tolerable. There was still the urge to vomit, but at least the pain had subsided. He rolled the empty glass in his hand thought of the word *pain*. An urge to break the edge off the glass rose in him, and just as it did, he saw a different word in his mind: *weapon*.

As the innkeeper had promised, an old square-shouldered man came to his side and spoke to him.

"David, how is your head?"

David palmed the glass.

"Fine."

96

"I saw you drink those shots."

David turned toward the stranger. "I said I'm fine. Who are you?"

"I'm Mr. Erelim."

"Doesn't help. Who are you?"

Mr. Erelim gave a small smile, one that was not reassuring but came across as a tool of pacification, thin and toothless. David's grip tightened on the glass. The smile faded from the older man's face and he said, "Join me outside, if you would. It's safer if we speak in private."

The men left the bar and stood in the alley. Erelim's hair was luminous in the shadows, almost as if possessing its own lighting filament. Holding his hand to his side, David clutched the glass. He felt he might crush through it. The points of light that reflected in the crevasses of the brick road blinked in his periphery and the world seemed to go liquid. David attempted to suppress his urge to vomit, but found himself spewing alcohol next to the old man's feet. The old man pulled from his jacket a syringe. David knocked it free from Erelim's hand. It shattered upon the ground. From the blurred fringes of his vision, blackened hands reached for him. There was a flash of steel, a shift of balance, and David had the henchman on the ground with his arm broken backwards at the elbow. Erelim stepped back. David pulled the knife from the henchman's hand, slit the throat, and walked toward Erelim.

David's steps were uncertain. The world had lost its definition. His stomach began to kick. A white flash from the corner of his eye and Erelim was upon him, deftly wrenching the blade from his hand. David landed the glass against the old man's brow as the first incision was made in his neck. Falling to the ground, with his hand upon the wound, David looked to the figure standing above him. Blood dripped from Erelim's brow.

"We had such hopes for you, David. You were our favorite."

The words flanged as they met David's ears. They too were losing definition.

"We've made some mistakes and we're correcting them now. It pains me to do this, son."

The shadows around them grew larger, falling upon him in a cloud. A cut to his hand to force it away, a cut to the throat. Air lost its way. Bubbled and hissed as he attempted to breathe. He made one last effort to undo the man and David was undone.

23

THREE FIGURES moved in battle. One emerged. Erelim. David attempted to quell his fear of the strange man. He'd have to follow him, but the thought of it made his skin itch. Erelim dropped something, wiped his hands, and walked into the light of the street. He looked in David's direction. David, worried that the whites of his eyes might be visible, closed them.

When David opened his eyes, the man was gone. *Follow*, came a voice. David dislodged himself from the dumpster and emerged from the alleyway. In the distance, the old man's hair served as a beacon. A small, wavering star. Managing to stay in the cover of shadows, David clung to the faces of buildings as best he could. When light fell on his skin, he saw his flesh bubble from beneath. "Not now," he whispered, and the landscape of his flesh fell still. He knew, however, that it would return. It would always return. Iosif said as much.

The shops and apartments that lined the streets leaned forward, threatening to collapse on him. Their bricked faces, adulterated by technologies, reflected no light but devoured it. Some areas in the city had clean buildings, painted white or yellow or pale gray but the north side lacked the optimism of those young neighborhoods, where children played in small courtyards and fathers planted honeysuckle bushes and cherry trees. The occasional hacked tree boles that punctuated the sidewalks were the only signifiers of some long ago time of progress. But they'd become blackened as well, as if petrified and immovable. It was a neighborhood of shadows.

Mr. Erelim moved between districts, shifting his route in strange unnatural ways, almost as if he expected a tail, but he never once turned his head to check. This pleased David, as he was unsure if his pursuit was inconspicuous. Some moments, when a sense of fear possessed him and he began to trail a bit farther behind, the voice would return to him. Again, not the voice of destruction and doubt, but the new voice. The voice of the bathroom. *Faster*, it would say, *faster*. He picked up his pace, hoping the man couldn't hear his shoes, his breath.

Mr. Erelim careened into a cul-de-sac of storage buildings. All of the warehouses at the far end of the street were fairly well lit; however, the structure in which the old man stopped was shrouded in night. Erelim stood and began rotating his neck as if trying to work free a knot. He bent at his knees and made an impressive jump to the last rung of a fire escape several feet above. Erelim pulled himself up the ladder, his body still, legs tight, until his feet reached the last rung and were able to aid in his ascent. David counted the floors. From his pocket he removed the pen. He exposed his forearm. A small mouth emerged from the cream of flesh. Another. Another. Soon, his skin percolated with grubs. Stabbing the pen into his flesh, he began to carve. One long line. A blazing ray of pain shooting through him. Two more. One parallel. One perpendicular. Biting against his lip, he tasted blood.

Run, a voice whispered. *Run.*

David found lifting his right foot difficult as if the ground beneath had sucked him into the concrete. Small grubs writhed as they fell. He pulled and labored against the ground. When his leg had broken free, he looked down to see there was no hole, no mark or crack. A stable alley. *Run*, came the voice. David ran.

THE SHELTER of drywall was still vacant, so David crept beneath. He began drawing a map, lines, squares, circles, and a star. He couldn't remember the street names very well but he remembered landmarks. A statue of a man on a bench, an old tree with a face carved into its bark, a building with neon stars, an alley with red dumpsters. It wasn't much, but it proved to him that he'd be able to remember the way if needed. Before long, his hands grew weak and his legs shook. He wrapped his arm in his shirttail and laid back.

The mists of half-dreams passed through his mind. The man with white hair. Launching off the fire escape. Sprouting wings. Their width majestic. Glinting silver feathers. Erelim swooping between buildings, snatching people that looked like David. Dropping them from lofty heights. Their bodies magically turning to red glitter upon impact. Then the world was flooded. A wave of water overtaking the streets. He found himself contained in a deprivation chamber. He made to breathe. The salty water filled his lungs.

Startled awake, David surveyed the square. Across the bricks, beyond the socialites walking to bars, he spied another man that looked like him. He and a woman with long blond hair stood by the entrance of the café. They didn't seem to say much. David pulled his collar around his neck; partially covering his face and traveling in right angles through the foot traffic, he crossed the court. When he was halfway across the arcade, a throng of tourists intercepted him. A woman holding a stick with a peach scarf tied at its end walked backwards and discussed the design of the city fountain. By the time he got near The Wilted Tulip, they'd vanished.

18

Low-lying clouds looked as if the sea had gone black and crawled above the city. No one was on the street and Saul was acutely aware of his own steps. From the rooftops, a bird called. He was not sure what type, but images of a crow came to mind and then the word *crow*. How long had it been since he'd seen a crow, or even seen a photograph of one? Not since his awakening. Saul had a sudden craving for alcohol. Something to wear the edges off of him, make the world soft and manageable.

When he'd given Merav enough time to make it to her home before him, Saul changed his direction and began navigating the streets, hoping he'd not lost himself in his convoluted stroll through the city. The word *city* formed itself in Saul's mind and he began to wonder if he'd ever been to another city. If he'd ever left this city, with its never ending streets and looming towers. All of the green spaces, hostages between bricks and pavement. Even the rogue flower blooms that attempted to reclaim life atop the sidewalk only did so through gaps in mortar.

As he rounded the corner, the light of the diner came into view. Merav's street. Following her instructions, Saul hid in the foyer of the apartment across the street. He stood there for a few minutes, a shadow among kin. No one walked the streets. No one followed him. Emerging from the dark, Saul crossed over to Merav's building. In the darkened entry, he nearly tripped over a man slipping into a pair of shoes much like his own.

"You startled me, mister."

The stranger looked up from beneath the brim of his hat and stared at Saul, his square jawline the only thing wholly visible in the gloom.

"You live here?" Saul asked.

The man grunted. Once his shoes were on, he locked eyes with Saul. Something about the look made Saul's skin grow hot around his ears.

"It's wet outside, best mind your step," Saul said, moving his hand carefully to his belt line.

The stranger put his hands in his pockets and gave a close-lipped smile. He stepped past Saul and into the street. With his gun in his hand, Saul hugged the doorframe and waited for the other to move on. When he saw the stranger's silhouette growing smaller against the lights of the diner, Saul walked up to Merav's apartment.

Merav greeted him with a drink and a kiss on the cheek. "Welcome," she said, her breath warm in his ear.

He took the drink from her and said, "I met one of your neighbors. A peculiar guy. Didn't say a word to me when I spoke to him. I'm guessing you and Uriah checked everyone out before you moved here."

She put her hands on the side of Saul's face and said, "I take it he didn't try to kill you."

Saul took a deep sip from his glass and said, "No."

Merav pulled back a few inches so that he could see her playful expression, "Then, relax. No one talks in this city. Besides, this is a city of strangers, Saul." She kissed him and he felt her tongue move inside him. She pulled the drink from him, let it crash to the floor, and led him into her bedroom.

17

HE AWOKE in his bed, fully clothed. In his right pocket, a note that read, *You are David. You were made in God's image. You are the author of all language, emender of sins.*

DAVID SAT on the edge of the bed. He wept. After passing the tears, he walked into the living room. There were matches on the coffee table. The matches were unused, each of them rested like children tethered to a bed. Their heads were white, coarse, cold. David wept. Between strained breaths, an image of a woman came to him. Blond, amber, black, her hair changed colors as she walked toward him. The tears came more freely. But why?

He perched on the corner of a leather sofa. Its rigid piping irritated the bend of his knee. Readjusting, he wiped his face clear of moisture. David tried to remember how he'd gotten to the hotel. All he could imagine was the woman with chameleon hair. Perhaps she'd brought him there. Certainly, he remembered her for a reason. Despite her changing colors, her face was remarkably clear to him. A symmetrical face. Sharp features.

A long, but attractive nose. Plum lipstick. She smoked, a haze of it washing her into the background.

Three knocks came at the door. David instinctively reached to his belt line. This made him want to cry again, but he held back. He took a deep breath and approached the door.

"Who is it?"

"David, it's Mr. Erelim. I'm here to see how you're feeling."

The voice, although markedly altered by the wood, was soft and familiar. As he slid the first lock open, David's heart began to palpitate. Sweat pushed through the pores in his back. He unlocked the final bolt and opened the door just wide enough to see a stout old man with white hair. Again, the urge to cry pushed against his throat.

"May I enter, friend?"

David coughed back his urge. "Yes, please."

Erelim entered with another, a large man with strange body modifications, perhaps tattoos. As the old man walked to a free chair, he said, "I apologize for the visit. It's not customary, but we've had to alter our operation due to time constraints." Mr. Erelim sat in a reading chair, David on the sofa.

"How are your crying spells?"

"I don't know. They're still here, I suppose. Where am I?"

"Your memory is gone completely?"

"Yes, but I keep thinking of a woman," David said, feeling his lips tremble with the word *woman*.

"Tell me about the woman."

"Where am I, Mr. Erelim?"

"More about the woman, David." The brow on the old man shifted, dipped, and returned to a neutral position. He smiled and continued, "I'm sorry. You're in a hotel. You live here."

"I live here? There are no personal effects."

Again, the man's brow shifted. Smiling once more, this time a little strained, Mr. Erelim said, "David, I need to know what you remember and then I can answer your questions."

This seemed a logical compromise. David said, "I don't know much about her. She's slender, smokes, has plum lips. She walks. No, she drifts. Her walk is like she's drifting, well-rehearsed. The strange thing is her hair changes colors."

He had her in his mind, then. A solid form, the smoke fading away. His heart was conflicted. At once, he wanted to smile and cry. He closed his eyes.

"Are you remembering?"

David smiled. Tears began to stream from beneath his blue-veined eyelids. "Yes," he said, "I see her clearly now. There's a dark room. She's leaning in to say something. I feel a sharp pain in my neck. It's going blurry." He stopped for a second and continued, "That's odd."

"What's odd, David?"

"Nothing."

"The mind has a strange way of telling you things. No matter how odd they are, your mind has seen them and reassembles them for you."

"I saw a mechanical spider and a spoked wheel."

"Yes."

"Then I saw you," David paused to swallow and then continued with a nervous laugh, "with a syringe."

"I'm sorry to hear this," Erelim said. "The longer you're exposed to the amnesic, the more unpredictable its effects become."

There was a shift in the atmosphere, then, as if the air

had grown heavy. The light grew dimmer and a searing tear crossed his neck. There was a wrist before him. Black with white markings. Tattoos.

It wasn't until David touched his neck that he realized he'd been murdered.

A small breath gurgled through the slit and the light gathered around Mr. Erelim before finally vanishing altogether.

18

THE EMBER of Merav's cigarette lit her face for a good second before the glow faded, taking her soft outline with it. Saul felt her breath in-between her ribs as she exhaled. His fingertips moved along the valleys of bone. Part of him wanted to push the tender flesh there, to see if she would smile. To hear her laugh.

"Yes, I've had other lovers," she said, "to answer your implied question. I stopped, though."

"Stopped dating or stopped having sex?"

"Questions, Saul."

"Yeah, right."

"Clearly, I've not stopped having sex. I've stopped having relationships. Dating. Whatever you'd like to call it. You shouldn't take it as an achievement, getting me in bed." She took another drag from her smoke. Her face born and erased by the same ember.

"Something made you stop."

"There was a time I was in love, Saul. The way I thought all people experienced love. We did things together. We walked holding hands. We spoke of love and futures and children. Still, I grew distant, he told me. He said he could sit in a room with me and feel a distance he'd not felt with strangers. I attempted to hold it together for some time. Sexy underwear. Gifts. Things women do. Things men seem to love. But it wasn't enough."

"He left."

"Yes. I thought I was okay with it. Then I grew quite morose. After a few months, I was happy to be done with the self-indulgent sulking about. It drove me mad. Months turned to a year. I ran into him and his fiancée somewhere. They were so natural, doing those things that couples do. Tickling, kissing, holding hands."

"You couldn't take his happiness."

"No. It wasn't that," she said, drawing, what Saul believed to be a long overdue, hit off her cigarette. "It's just that I was never like that. That soft, loving type. The wake up in the morning and breakfast together type. I decided not to date after that. I'd seek only pleasure. My pleasure." She sighed and continued, "Then, I met Mr. Uriah."

Saul conjured up the chair. He thought about the face. There was only flesh.

"He's your focus now. Allowing you empathy without the mess of romance."

She inhaled. "Something like that."

"I'd like to know how you met."

Merav gave a small laugh and kissed him on the forehead. "You would like to know so much."

"A man born in mystery is a man who must search for answers."

Merav kissed him on the mouth. "I was his caretaker for a time. I heard a lot of things, then. Things that I didn't think I was meant to hear, but know now that I was. Eventually, I began asking questions."

"I take it, he answered them."

"Much in the manner he answers your questions. Over time, the pieces came together. He's a brilliant man. I had nothing before I worked for him. I was living a meaningless existence. Drifting. Seducing men at bars, slipping away with their billfolds at the end of the night. Mr. Uriah brought me into the fold as he understood I had certain," she rubbed Saul's arm, "attributes that men find difficult to resist."

"How did you come under his employ?"

"One night I allowed a very rich doctor to take me home. He caught me with my hand in his wallet. He grabbed my wrist and I pulled my penknife on him. He gave me the strangest smile, as if pleased. He released me and asked me if I was interested in making an honest living."

"Odd you consider this an honest living."

Pushing her cigarette into a crystal ashtray, she said, "The most honest."

"Tell me the reason you chose me at the bar."

"I didn't choose you."

"I must have been chosen for a reason."

"Saul, these things have been in play for longer than I know. I may be Mr. Uriah's assistant, but I don't have the answers you're looking for."

"It seems that would grow frustrating."

"Trust is earned, dear." Merav shifted atop the sheet. Her body's shape barely visible in the night.

"Tell me why I can't remember anything."

"As far as we can tell, they inject something into you. You usually go back to your room and one night you'll disappear for a while. When you come back, there's this curve where we have to identify, observe, and reeducate you."

"Tell me my purpose."

"I can't tell you that, Saul."

"You mean you won't even if you could."

Merav touched his shoulder. "Mr. Uriah must tell you when he thinks it's time. There are some answers I simply don't know."

"I don't know if that's good enough for me, Merav," Saul said, moving his legs off the side of the bed.

She placed her hands on his back, crept behind him, wrapped her arms around his chest and kissed his ear. "Things are changing, love. You'll soon know what you need. Let me convince you to stay," she said, pulling him back, crawling atop him.

Saul laughed, perhaps a bit too honestly. "A woman with confidence is a dangerous thing," he said. He wasn't sure but he believed he felt her smile while she kissed his stomach. Again, he decided this would be as fine as any ending and chose to stay.

30

IT WAS nearly noon by the time David's marks emerged from the apartment. First, the woman, and after a half an hour, the man. David exited the car and followed at a distance. It was nice to be outside, to feel the stretch of walking. In the daylight, the city acted differently. Instead of folding in and threatening to collapse into the streets, the buildings seemed to shimmer, capture light and share it. The sun broke through the dim sheath of clouds for a minute. A mural of a matador with mirrored embellishments on his coat, sparkled with a fiery hubris that made David want to shoot the light from the sky. However, the clouds shifted and the corona was obscured once again.

Saul was cautious, turning and backtracking. Erelim was right: the man had come into his own. There were moments when David was sure the man was onto him. David hid in shadows, let Saul get well ahead of him, cut through alleys to hide, and eventually found himself a bit lost. Had it not been for the fortuitous event that Saul nearly bumped into him at a busy intersection, David would have surrendered his search and returned to the car.

When Saul looked at him, his face was slack with the

undeniable look of indifference. Perhaps the lack of lighting in the hallway had obfuscated the stranger's view. David saw it as a sign from God. Yet, as he faced the man, the flow of pedestrians wrapping around them, it was clear that something was wrong. He didn't recognize David. Something inside him shifted. If he'd known better, he might call it joy.

Raising his hand toward the street, David signaled for the other to cross before him.

"Thank you," the other said.

David gave a slight tip of his fedora.

With only a few steps between them, David followed for several more blocks until the street ended and the sidewalk poured into the delta of the town center. David couldn't help himself—he inched closer. Not so close as to be obvious, but close enough that a thrill of excitement coursed through him. His hands begged to twist the man's neck. To feel it snap.

As they walked past the fountain, David saw Merav sitting at a table outside a café. When he ascertained that Saul was moving across the walkway to meet with her, he stepped away and took a seat at a bakery caddie corner to The Wilted Tulip.

A waiter came and placed a menu on the table. David cut his eye toward the aproned man and then back toward the menu. In a tidy script, a list of baked goods and chocolates were listed. Running his finger down the page, past the Danishes, the tarts, the cakes, he found a list of pies and pointed to blueberry. He then moved his finger to the right column and double tapped to indicate he wanted a personal pie and not simply a slice.

Merav and Saul sat across from one another and drank wine. Saul took his first sip and made a disapproving face. The woman laughed and signaled for the waiter. He could kill them both from where he sat. A bullet first in the man, and then another in the woman as she sat, stunned.

The waiter came with his pie. The crust was thick and sprinkled over with large granules of sugar. David pierced the flesh of it with his fork, pulling back a mound of sweetened blueberries. Steam rose and expired. He'd not finished swallowing his first forkful before he'd shoveled another in, repeating until the pie was nearly finished.

A child stood on the corner. His face to the sky. Mouth agape. His shaggy black hair bunched beneath an Irish flat cap. He spun several times and came to a halt, causing his curly black hair to tremble. Slowly, he lowered his chin until his eyes met with David's. As if in a trance, the boy's body moved forward. Pedestrians labored to miss him. His mission was uncompromised. When he arrived at David's table, he pulled a dead pigeon from the pocket of his tiny suit coat. The wind teased the broken feathers jutting between the boy's cupped fingers.

"This is yours," the boy said.

David shook his head.

The boy tossed the small corpse at him and said, "You're a bad man."

The pigeon hit his shoulder and tumbled forward onto his plate. Its eyeless head made pillow on a gout of blueberry filling. The boy stood there, his focus trained on David, who removed his gun and sat it on the table. With a gasp, the kid ran back to the opposite side of the street, where his grandmother met him with comeuppance for his wandering, boxing him about the ears with her clutch purse.

Without moving, David studied the bird, its gorey sockets glinting among the fruit. There was something terrible about its stare—the lack of difference in its appearance living or dead. He tossed his napkin over it and looked up in time to see Saul and Merav hailing a cab. David left several bills at his table and walked closer to the couple at The Wilted Tulip.

18

"PULL OVER at this church."

"I thought we were going back to my place, Saul."

"I need to see a priest."

Merav's left eyelid twitched just below the slit. Saul put his hand on her thigh, leveled his head and said, "Don't worry yourself. I'm still in the old man's corner for now, but we're being followed."

Merav checked the back window and said, "How do you know?"

"There is a man in a taxi trailing us. He left the cafe when we did."

"I should go with you."

"We both know that's a bad idea."

The driver cruised into a loading zone and Saul left. Slipping into the shadows of the cathedral, he spied the other cab tailing him park. When he got a good look at the guy, he entered the building and found a verger lighting candles in the prayer room.

"I'm looking for a priest. Last name Tentorio."

"He's in the back room preparing for reconciliations. May I ask who's calling?"

Saul pulled the angel card from his pocket and said, "Just give him this. He'll know."

As he waited for the priest, Saul kept watch over the entrance. Whoever was tailing him was savvy enough not to walk into a deserted church. Voices came from behind him and he turned around to find an old priest instructing another verger to prepare the confessional. The priest approached, held up the card, and smiled.

"My friend, I'm so happy you've come to see me."

Saul greeted the old man with a handshake. "Thanks for seeing me, Father."

"Not an issue. I'm always happy to talk, but I must admit that today I'm a bit short on time as it's a day of reconciliation for many of our parishioners. You wouldn't by chance be here for confessional?"

"No."

Tentorio raised his head a bit, his mouth slightly open. "What can I do for you, friend?"

"Father, do you have a place where we could speak privately?"

"Nothing," the priest said, "is more private than the confessional booth, but there's a catch."

"What's that?"

"You'll have to confess something. A sin."

"I'm not a religious man."

"Ah, friend, just because you're not listening to the Lord, doesn't mean that He's not listening to you. What's your name?"

"Saul."

Repeating the name, Tentorio pointed toward the confessional booths. "Shall we?"

The men entered the booth, Saul in one door and Tentorio in the other. Through the thin wooden screen that separated them, Saul could just make out the shape of the priest, but his features were adulterated.

"What is it that you have come here for?"

"I've learned something about the people who left me this card and I want to get your thoughts on it."

"I'm listening, son."

"They have several people they're keeping tabs on. A militia of twins."

The priest gave a sigh, one that indicated not much of anything but enough to put Saul off his words.

"Is my story tiring you, Father?"

"I'm not here to judge you. It's your reconciliation."

"It's not my damned reconciliation. I'm here to get your thoughts."

Father Tentorio apologized for his interruption and said, "When you say people, whom exactly do you mean?"

"The Council of the New Mystical Body."

Father Tentorio gave a small moan before asking, "New Mystical Body? Are you sure they said the New Mystical Body?"

"Yeah. What's it mean?"

"I'm not sure exactly. It still smacks of a Catholic reformation sect to me. The Church frequently deals with these things, people taking bits of one philosophy or another and cobbling together a manifesto. It would make sense. The re-appropriation of the angel on that card you showed me." Tentorio paused as if to collect a thought but redirected, "How are you involved in this?"

"I'm told I've been an inside operative for some time."

"I'm confused, Saul. You say this as if you didn't know it."

"I don't remember much. A long sleep, but nothing before."

"A long sleep?"

"Yes."

"Are you an amnesiac?"

"Would I know?"

The priest laughed. "I guess not."

Saul searched through the mesh to read the man's face.

"What's the earliest memory you can recall?"

"Waking in a hotel room several days ago. I went to a bar and met a woman named Merav and she took me to an old man."

"Are these the people who told you about the others?"

"Yes."

"How do they know these things?"

Saul considered his phrasing. What might sound reasonable. If he says everything, Tentorio will think he's mad. "The old man used to be a part of the Council. He lost his faith and now he's trying to stop them. He believes they're up to something big."

"What exactly?"

"I'm not sure. There are things they've yet to tell me."

"Why do you trust these people?"

"I don't."

"But you still listen to them?"

Saul put his hand on the edge of his chin, rubbed. "They're the only people providing me with answers."

"You're not asking the right questions, Saul. It seems that they are only providing you with selective answers." The priest thought for several seconds, his breath slow and deliberate. "You look about for too much outside help."

Something pricked the back of Saul's mind. He instinctively clinched his fist and said, "What the hell does that mean?"

Tentorio leaned in and for the first time his face was clear among the mesh. "Are you upset?"

"I've grown weary of the mystery, Father."

Tentorio eased back, his face once again obscured by the mesh. "I'm sure you have. I know the type of person you're describing and you're not thinking objectively about them."

"What does that mean?"

"Let me tell you an old story: a young man searching for spiritual guidance approaches a road which trifurcates. At the end of each of these roads lay a building. The first building is made of glistening steel, the second of marble, and the third a dilapidated slat-wood house. The young man goes first to the metallic building, as its lofty metal spire impresses him. When he arrives at the door, he is greeted by a man in a white robe. The man welcomes the young traveler and asks him to come into his building. As they step through the threshold, the traveler sees that there are wires and cables running along the walls, great veins connected to a glowing orb above a pulpit. 'What is that orb in the west window?' the traveler asks. The man in the white robe smiles and replies, 'The orb is Tesla's Plasma Lamp, the light that guides modern man.' The young man asks, 'Do you then worship Tesla?' The man in white replies, 'We follow only the path of truth.' The traveler asks the man if he can tell him the meaning of life and the man replies, 'To answer that which we once thought was unknowable.' The young man thanks the man in white for his generosity and says that he will continue. As he turns to leave, the man in white says, 'When you turn your back on reason, you will find yourself paralyzed by fear and helplessness.' The young man steps back into the sunlight and the door slams behind him, several locks thrumming closed.

"The traveler walks then to the marble structure. This building is older and grander than the one previous. He marvels at the carefully laid flying buttresses and the magnificent rose window on the eastern wall. He approaches two entrance doors, nearly three times his height. Here, an older man welcomes him. The young man asks if he might come inside and see the building. The man, a preacher dressed in red robes, says that the young man must first atone for everything his forefathers had done and cleanse himself of the sins of his father. The traveler asks if he can first see the building, as the previous man had been kind enough to let him inside. The preacher slams his hand hard against the thick wooden doors and yells, 'The way of the flesh shall never pervert the sanctity of the church! Repent and you shall gain entry.' The young traveler backs away and hurries along to the third structure he'd seen in the distance.

"When he arrives to the small house, he finds that the door is open and so he walks through the threshold. There are no ornate statues or stain glass windows. He walks to a chair just below an empty pulpit and finds a feeble old man sitting alone, his back craning forward, weak and thin. The young traveler places his hand on the man's back. 'Sir,' he says, 'are you unwell?' The old man looks up from his hands and smiles. 'No,' he says, 'I am just resting. Why have you come here, son?' 'I am on a path to discover my purpose,' the young traveler replies. 'Is this your house?' 'A man does not own in this lifetime, he simply borrows until he passes and I am soon to pass,' the old man says. The young man asks, 'What will happen then?' The old man says, 'Someone will come just as I did and just as you have now and he will occupy this space. Someone always does.' 'Do you want me to believe that I've been sent to take your place?' the young man asks. The old man looks at him, his eyes sparkling in the dim sunlight, 'Son,' he says, 'one should never trust a man who tells him what to believe.' The traveler finds another chair and sits next to the old man. 'Maybe,' he says, 'I'll just stay here for a little while and make sure you're okay.'"

Father Tentorio stopped and waited for Saul to speak.

"What the hell is that supposed to mean?" Saul asked.

"Think on it for a while, Saul."

A knock came at the confessional door.

"I have to see to my flock now. I'd like to meet with you after you've thought about it. I'll be at the bar tonight."

"You shouldn't drink so much, Father."

Tentorio laughed. "Allow me some earthy pleasure, son."

Saul looked at his hands. They were larger than he remembered, strong and coarse. He began to leave the booth.

"Wait, Saul," Tentorio said.

"Yes, Father."

"Your confession."

Saul thought to leave, but wasn't one to welch on a deal. He smoothed his hair and said, "I had relations with a woman out of wedlock."

Father Tentorio said, "I'd ask you to say some prayers but I know you won't. I'll pray for you and hope God hears my prayers. God be with you, my son."

"Yeah."

SAUL LEFT the church. He'd grown dry and walked to The Wilted Tulip. The barista, a young man with rolled shirtsleeves, greeted him and Saul ordered water. When it arrived, he took it in a swallow. His body, slow to process, demanded more and so he ordered. A couple sat at the window. The man with his hand on the knee of the other. He spoke into her ear and she laughed, lolling her head back, her black ponytail shaking from her collared blouse and swinging behind her. He thought about Merav's past lover. How she must have felt. Saul took another sip of the water, letting it stay on the bend of his tongue for a bit longer. When it had fallen toward his stomach, he said the word *love*. It was a strange word. A word whose image he could not conjure. Something about the thought put him off of going to Merav's house and so he stepped into the night and walked the dark streets, rolling the priest's story around in his head.

The city unfurled beneath his feet; Saul began to see things in a different light. It was as if the streets had been redesigned or the buildings around him had altered, as if a movie crew had erected a wood-thin set while he'd been away. He noticed statues he'd not recalled seeing, fountains that never spit water, bike racks littered with too many bicycles on every street. He had been directed by someone since he awoke. First, the note and matches, then Merav and Mr. Uriah. He'd admittedly been foggy since the awakening, and, as Mr. Uriah himself had pointed out, Saul was coming back into his own, whatever, he thought, that meant. The priest raised a valid point. Saul needed to ask better questions and seek out his own answers.

30

DAVID SAT across from Mr. Erelim in a dark room, a lamp scarcely lighting the ground directly beneath them. A blackened arm emerged from that blurred edge of light with a drink. David accepted it but didn't break eye contact with Erelim. When the man served Erelim, gin with a wedge of lime, the old man smiled and took breath to speak.

"What did you learn today?"

David handed Mr. Erelim his notes. He read them slowly, his eyebrows raising from time to time, occasionally licking at the lime with the side of his tongue, moving it around the edge of the glass. It was the most human thing David had ever seen him do. He, in turn, took a drink of his whiskey. He rattled the ice against the glass by accident, rousing Erelim's attention away from the notes.

"This priest could be trouble," Erelim said.

David agreed.

"Did anyone see you?"

David shook his head.

Saul had yet to recognize him. When a man recognizes another, the facial muscles give him up.

"Your answer was hesitant," Erelim said.

David shook his head again, perhaps too quickly.

"You may deal with this priest in the future if you feel it necessary." Erelim gave a toothy smile and said, "There is a task on which I need your assistance. I only trust you enough to help."

David chose not to nod but to take a deliberate and slow drink from his glass. A move he hoped would put Erelim off of any more questions about Saul. When he had finished with his whiskey, a servant came and collected the glass.

Mr. Erelim stood. "Let us go, then."

They snaked through the alleyways and along walkways between buildings. It was a rather long walk across the lower end of town, far beyond any street David had traveled in recent memory. He began to wonder if there was a reason for this, if Mr. Erelim wasn't setting him up. He kept his hand on his piece, listened behind him for steps, lagged behind a couple feet when they neared corners.

Once they arrived at a large hotel that looked much like the Hotel South, Mr. Erelim turned and spoke, "This is the new hotel. Your brothers will sleep here now."

David nodded, his hand at the ready.

This was not lost on Erelim, who smiled and said, "David, I am not bringing you to your end. If I wanted you murdered, you'd be dead already. We've been seeing to the decommissioning of all unsuccessful operatives. You will be our last man standing."

They walked around the building and entered. It was a nicer place. A proper concierge, a lounge with reading materials, and a boy minding the elevator. It unsettled David.

All of the Maya for the downfall of man. He hoped that he would not be transferred. His room suited him well. Following Erelim, David found himself at the door of a room on the sixth floor. Mr. Erelim knocked thrice and a man who looked like David answered.

"Hello," he said, "I was wondering when you'd arrive."

"I was delayed," Mr. Erelim replied.

The man let them into the room and studied David. As they took their seats, he didn't notice that Mr. Erelim hadn't sat at all, but had walked around the couch and stood just behind him.

"How are the aches?"

The man on the couch answered, "Mostly they've grown better with the medicine you gave me."

"This is good," Mr. Erelim said. "Were you in contact with the new counterfeiter?"

"Yes, he's agreed to notify me if anyone should come in with a card."

"For fear or profit?"

The man smiled and said, "You can't trust a man interested in profit, can you?"

Mr. Erelim agreed with him and injected a needle into his neck before the man on the couch realized what had happened. He struggled for a few seconds but fell limp.

"I'll need your help getting him into a cab," Mr. Erelim said.

David did as he was asked. When the man was in the cab, Mr. Erelim instructed the cabbie and said, "My friend's brother, here, had too much to drink in the bar." He handed the driver a business card and said, "This one's mute, so you'll not get a word out of him. Take them to that address and the doorman will pay you."

The cabbie looked back. "You ain't coming? There's room in the front."

Mr. Erelim's lips drew flat along his face. He shook his head and said, "I always choose to walk. It's good for the constitution."

He shut the door and the taxi pulled away. They sat in traffic for some time. Whenever the stranger moved in his sleep, David worried that he'd have to kill him in the back of the cab. This would mean he'd have to kill the driver as well. It would be a tricky maneuver in the best of circumstances, let alone canned in-between one hundred witnesses during a traffic jam. He considered the possibilities as the sun cut around a building and lay upon the stranger's face, revealing all facial similarities. The other had more lines along his brow. More sun color to his skin. Were they the same age, he wondered. If only he could cut him open like a tree to count the rings. Then it occurred to David that he didn't know his own age. Is this, he wondered, something that a man needed to know? A life was not measured in years but in his service. Service to himself and to God. The man gritted his teeth. David watched the muscle work beneath the skin, a snake wanting to be birthed.

By the time they reached their destination, the sun had fallen beneath the buildings and was well on its way to vanishing behind the horizon just beyond the river. The cab driver asked David if the fare was going to be paid, but stopped short when a man in white exited the building and came to the window with cash in hand. David maneuvered the body out of the backseat and began to drag him to the door when the man in white laid a hand on his shoulder. Without thought, David dropped the dead weight and had his gun at the other's temple.

"Mr. Erelim," the man began, "wants you to wait here. I will carry this guy."

David didn't move. He leaned into the temple a bit more. The other turned his head, his eyes wide like a dog in a trap. Despite his urge to pull the trigger, David saddled his gun. The man in white backed away with caution, pulling the unconscious man from the ground. The struggle to get him to the entrance of the building was clumsy. Angling the other against his shoulder, the man in white removed a key card from his pocket. He slipped it into a metal box, waited, and removed it when the door opened. Within a few steps, he was inside the building and the door locked behind him.

18

SAUL WAITED at the bar for some time before the priest arrived. Tentorio bellied up next to him and signaled for a beer, after which he turned to him and said, "I hope you don't mind, but I've asked a fellow priest to join us."

"Why?"

"He's a scholar and the local authority on Catholic cults. Don't worry, I didn't tell him anything, just that there was someone I'd like for him to meet."

"I'm not sure I want to meet anyone, Father."

"Understandable. But if anyone knows something about your people, it'll be Father Jonathan. Tell him what you'd like. Or," Tentorio said as he received his beer, "nothing at all."

They sat for a time without saying a word, drinking and listening to the sounds of the bar. A couple in the corner arguing over semantics. A man at the far side of the bar telling a stranger a tale of how he'd lost his arm in the Great War. A homely woman standing at a table singing some horrible radio hit to herself. Glasses rattled as the bar-back gathered empties between his fingertips. It was the cacophony of nightlife in the city that constantly folded in upon itself. The sound of the city, awake. Breathing in clicks and clatter.

Eventually, Saul spoke, "Fine, I'll meet your man."

Tentorio lips flattened into a long, thin smile.

"I got your message, Father."

"How's that, son?"

"The parable. Its point wasn't lost on me. I just prefer people be direct."

"As a priest, I'm prone to parable."

Saul took a drink and said, "Parable and bullshit."

Tentorio laughed, "Trained on the former, born into the latter, I'm afraid. I suppose I should rethink my approach."

A short, dark haired man in a black overcoat entered the bar as Tentorio looked down into his drink processing some bit of memory or another. Saul examined the man as he surveyed the patrons. His face, squat like a pumpkin, and lemon-colored like Chiffon, tensed as he squinted against the foggy lights, making his appearance all the more inhuman. The mist outside had slicked his skin, leaving him damp as a baby in placenta. The short man raised his hand and headed toward Saul, who turned to face the priest, only to realize that Tentorio was waving the newcomer to the bar.

"Saul, this is Father Jonathan. Or would you prefer to be called Doctor Jonathan?"

"I put duty before vanity, my friend," Jonathan said, his voice nasally and bubbled down in phlegm. "It's a pleasure to meet you, Saul," he said. He coughed to clear his throat and followed by extending his hand, a claggy ham hock that came alive with spidery fingers.

Saul looked at it, waiting a beat or two, and finally took it in his. "Can I buy you a drink, Father?"

"Aye," he said, "I'll have the same as Tentorio."

Saul swiveled around gently and ordered the man a drink. As the priests spoke to one another about a matter relating to the rectory, Saul wiped his hand clean with a napkin. Even when he'd done this, it felt heavy and strange. The bartender brought the beer, its head easing over the brim and along the edge. Jonathan wiped the side of the drink with his finger, which he pulled into his mouth in a displeasing suck. Turning to his own drink, Saul weighed his options. Tentorio was a decent man, probably the only man he trusted. What did that amount to? He barely trusted himself anymore. Where at first he'd thought the world was an unfolding carnation, he now was beginning to think that it was dying, the tender petals brown and hardened, falling in on him. He would be buried alive in their mystery, in the secret darkness and the imposing walls that seemed inescapable.

"Father Tentorio says you have something you'd like to show me."

The voice had come so suddenly, it took Saul several moments to realize that Father Jonathan was speaking to him. He felt the card in his pocket and took a slow deliberate drink.

"Yes." He removed the card, not revealing it at first, but deciding to do so after watching Tentorio.

Jonathan's eyes widened just enough to send a bolt of worry into Saul's gut. The priest slid the card from Saul's hand and said, "I've seen this angel before. Yes, I've seen it."

Tentorio, drank his beer and looked on in an odd sense of wonder.

"Would you like to hear about it?"

"That's why I'm showing it to you."

The priest smiled and said, "Saul, you're the type who only knows how to fall headlong into trouble, you know that?"

"How's that?"

"Your manner's all wrong, son. You're pricks and kicks and wouldn't understand decorum if it handed you a damned greeting card."

"Niceties aren't part of my job description, Padre."

"Nonetheless, a man could learn something from a little give and take."

"Father, I don't know you and I'm only talking to you because Tentorio vouched for you. Offending your delicate sensibilities isn't on my list of concerns. Are you going to tell me what you know or am I going to have to walk out of here and leave you with my tab? I promise you it's not slight."

"Oh, praise Jesus," Jonathan said, "I'm paid a miserable stipend; I best tell you all I know." He signaled for another beer and said, "I'm adding my tab to yours. Consider it a travel fee." Then he laughed and gave a wink.

"You drive a hard bargain," Saul said, loosening his expression and working a small grin onto his mouth.

As the beer made it to the table, Jonathan began, "As a young scholar, I began my studies, focusing on rebellion within the Church, rebellion and reform. You must understand that most of the classes offered in this specialization are created as a means to prevent another Luther, Zwingli, or Calvin. To me, the big three weren't the most fascinating areas of study. Certainly, they had the most resounding long-term effects on the Church, but I found the smaller groups to be of more interest." Jonathan looked around the bar in such a way that made it difficult to determine if he was following his own train of thought, or just paranoid. "A handful of us began hosting reading groups in our rooms to pursue our own interests as our elders were not keen on the idea of students objectifying challengers of the Papacy. It was wonderful at first, but many of my study-mates got hung up on the Knights Templar, which, as interesting a history as that may be, is well covered. I began looking into other groups. Groups thought long gone."

Tentorio interjected, "I'm interested to know where you find books on this sort of thing." His eyelids peeled tightly back into the sockets, his lips slick with beer.

"There's not much written on them. I spent much of my free time tracking down pamphlets and tracts. I had an excellent book trader in London and I'd make the voyage over there from time to time while studying in Dublin. During my dissertation year, I spent my time divided between my official dissertation research and my personal research. I was supposed to be in Italy studying, but I was not. I was everywhere else. I had a mate in Italy who would mail letters for me to keep up the appearances that I was where I was meant to be."

Jonathan moved the card in his hand. Fingered the delicate engraving. "But this card is unique. Modern. I've never seen something quite like it," he said, wiping his nose with is sleeve. "Older versions of this particular symbol, I have seen before though."

"So you know the group," Saul said.

"Not exactly, but I'm not ruling out that a radical faction exists."

Tentorio stood and tapped his fingers on the bar. "Well, don't say anything I don't know, I've got to hit the head."

Jonathan watched him walk away. He leaned in a bit too closely and said, "Would you mind lending me the card? I could look into it for you."

Saul took the card back and slipped it into his pocket. "I think I'll hang onto it."

Jonathan faced the bar and said, "There's an engraving of Rogziel on one of the buildings near the mid-town hospitals. I don't think it'd be a waste of your time to go down there and poke around a little."

"Probably not," Saul said and finished the last of his gin. "Maybe I'll swing by the church tomorrow after I check it out."

Three men approached the bar. Two of them ordered drinks and the third tried to slip behind Saul but there wasn't enough room between his back and the wall.

"Are you going to let Father Tentorio through?" Jonathan asked.

Saul turned to look at the man trying to slip by him. He examined his face but couldn't make him out as Tentorio. "I'm sorry, Father. I thought you were with them."

He leaned forward slightly, giving him wide enough berth.

"Not an issue, my friend," Tentorio said, easing by.

Without looking, Jonathan said, "Seems like you didn't recognize Tentorio there."

"What?"

"Are you sure that was Tentorio you let by just now?"

Saul looked at the two men to his left and then back to Tentorio. He could register no differences in the men's faces. All three appeared the same to him. He examined the attire. Tentorio wore a black button down, the men wore white.

Jonathan glowered into the distance, as if watching the bartender, but he wasn't. He was looking past him to some space that only Jonathan could see, a thought metastasizing in the smoke.

Jonathan said, "Nothing like a good beer. Eh, Father?"

"I agree," Tentorio said before humming some love song from his youth, that time before the war, gone now and scarcely remembered by anyone.

The bartender came to them. "Can I get you gentlemen anything else?"

Jonathan said, "You got nuts?"

"What?"

"Nuts."

"Do we serve nuts?"

"That's what I asked."

"No."

"Pretzels?"

"Pretzels?"

"Are you slow, son?"

"No, Father."

"Do you have pretzels?"

"Excuse my friend," Tentorio said.

"For what?" said Jonathan.

"For being rude."

Jonathan took a drink of his beer.

The bartender was unnerved, his eyes spread in worry. He turned his attention to Saul and said, "Another gin, sir?"

"I'm good, pal." He slipped the kid money for the tab and another couple bills to ease him on Jonathan's unwarranted abuse.

"Thanks for your help, Father Jonathan," Saul said, keeping careful eye on the priest's actions.

"My pleasure," Jonathan said without looking back.

Tentorio bolted to his feet, a bit off balance, but not enough to topple. "Let me walk you out, Saul." When they'd stepped outside, Tentorio asked, "What did you learn?"

"That your friend has a hell of a bedside manner."

"What do you mean?"

"It's no matter, friend. I'm going to check a couple places he suggested."

"Please do. I'd like to hear what you discover. I'll be in confession most of tomorrow, but if you're in the mind, do swing by." Tentorio's eyes were bright, his lips nearly liquid. It was the look of unfiltered kindness. Something Saul couldn't place as ever having seen before.

"I don't know how you do it, Father. All that talking and listening."

"It's my service to God, Saul."

Saul found himself slipping a few bills toward the priest.

"I have no need for this."

"Do what you will with it, Father."

"I'll donate it to the Church."

"Do what you will."

23

DAVID DREAMT again in a brief moment of sleep. He was in a tub of pale viscous fluid. There were wires attached to him. Somewhere in the distance something hissed and pumped rhythmically. Though his eyes were bandaged, he could make out lights and darks and vague shapes. He was consciously dreaming but could not control his body. He tried to stand. Tried to move his arms. To speak.

Footsteps birthed from the din of background noise. They grew louder and closer and soon someone was behind him. Wake, he thought, wake. Yet he did not. The man behind him spoke a language that seemed to manifest only in his dreams. Sharp and angular. A language unfriendly to song. The man dropped a metal clipboard, startling David. His dream body gave a tremor, the liquid sucking and popping along the edges of the tub.

"Anti-thesis jetset! Dry undirty."

David tried to understand the meaning behind it. Was it code? His body trembled as if it knew something David didn't and, in fact, it did, as only moments later, another man entered the room and pricked David with a needle. The men, cloaked in silhouette, spoke, but they faded and David's dream grew dark.

He awoke in an alley behind a diner. A dishwasher was tossing broken glasses into a dumpster. He pulled a paper-wrapped donut from his apron.

"I was gonna eat it later, but it looks like you could use it more than me."

David took the package and gave thanks. He unwrapped it and examined the donut, the yellow neon cabaret sign abstracting in the glaze. A dim choir of voices began to kick-up inside him. Closing his eyes against the noise, he pulled the baked good to his mouth and took a bite. Working it between his teeth was difficult. He'd grown so weak, forgotten to eat for too long. It was all he could manage to swallow. A woman's voice rose from those inside his head. *Don't eat*, she said, *you'll feed them. Feed them all.* His skin began to itch. To prickle. Again, he chewed at the sweet dough, trying his best to ignore the advice.

In the dark of his thoughts, he began to envision himself standing in the alley, eating, shivering, maggots dripping from him and curling into tight rings upon the grease-stained pavement. It began to turn his stomach. He thought of Ileana, but couldn't remember her face. He could only see a flesh balloon draped with soft dark curls of hair. Then the head began to pulsate, swell, and finally it split open, rife with grubs.

David bent over, vomited. Mostly bile. Bits of dough. Dropping the food, he stumbled out of the alley and made his way back into the streets, careful to avoid drawing attention to himself. By the time he'd shaken off the sick, he was deep into the mid-town business district. The last time he'd been there was when he followed the man with white hair. David sought shelter. When he'd found a pile of discarded appliance boxes, he constructed a small room and snaked his way in. He was nearly comfortable when he saw another David walk past. The man looked to the sky and then to something in his hand. He moved down the avenue a bit further, looked to the sky and then to his hand. He did this once more and then made his way right.

David wriggled from his makeshift fort and followed. As he turned the corner, the other David was looking around the doorframe of one of the buildings. David slid between two dumpsters and watched. *Don't go any closer*, a voice called. He couldn't tell if he should listen to the advice. Although it was a softer, like the voices in the bus depot, the other voices were catching on. Emulating. They were becoming seductive. Beseeching him in the darkling hours of night to cut into his flesh and dig free the infected meat. To toss out his food. They were trying to kill him.

18

SAUL EXAMINED the security box on the wall. It wasn't similar to anything he'd seen before; however, it occurred to him that he may have seen something like it before but simply couldn't remember. There was so much he couldn't account for in his life. Pulling the calling card from his breast pocket, he eased it into the slot. It wouldn't take. He flipped it a few times and eventually found the proper direction. The door clicked, electricity buzzing somewhere inside its frame. The doorknob turned with little resistance so he pulled it open and peeked inside. When it seemed clear that no one was guarding the entrance, Saul eased his way in, closing it quietly behind him. He gave the knob a twist to ensure he could exit freely and crept into the hallway.

In the distance, machines made unfamiliar noises. Hiss and moan. Saul walked down the hallway checking locks until he found a pair of swinging doors that opened at the touch. Pulling his gun free, he nosed forward. Surgical lamps and hospital beds lined the room, yet it was pitch as night save for a brilliant light that bled from the bottom crack of a doorway. It was on the other side of the door that Saul could hear someone speaking. He couldn't decipher the words. Inching closer, Saul was startled by the sudden sniff of a man sleeping in one of the beds.

Crouching down, he waved an arm to see if the man was awake. When the sleeper didn't speak, Saul crept to the door and opened it just enough to see inside. In the distance, a man with a lab coat labored over a utility sink, his back turned to the door. Twenty feet from Saul was a row of tubs with cables running into machines with lights and switches and rolls of paper. As he was about to slip inside the door, a body shot up from the bathtub closest to him. Gasping and covered in some type of gelatinous ooze, the man attempted to pull the wires free from his head and chest, frantic and blind. The man at the sink turned and faced the door.

"Halt!"

Saul let the door shut and made for the exit. As he ran through the room, the surgical lamps switched on in sequence. The sleeping man awoke and attempted to get out of bed but fell onto the floor, limp and floundering. Saul put his aim on the man but it wasn't as if the man was even aware of his presence. Like the man was an infant just hatched from some unspeakable womb. By the time Saul made it back to the exit, he could hear several men running down the hallway. Just before the door snapped shut, Saul dove and crawled beneath a parked loading truck.

From the ground, he watched as three men emerged. One checked around the corner and the other two spoke in hushed voices. When the first returned, they went back inside. It seemed that they weren't too concerned about finding him. It struck him as strange and thus he stayed hidden for a while longer.

Hours passed before his body began to ache. First along his abdomen and then in brilliant rays along his thighs and shins. Despite the sleep that had collected in his calves, Saul crept out from beneath the rig and left. A scraping noise arose from the back of the alley. Saul turned to survey the area but found nothing. He walked onto the main street and headed north, losing himself in the sea of pedestrian traffic.

SAUL HAD the feeling someone was following him but no matter how many ways he tried to force the tail to reveal himself, he would not, so he wandered in public venues for some time, often losing himself among throngs of tourists shuffling about in groups, looking at the spires and statutes of the city. Eventually, he went into a bar and drank a gin. When it was half way empty, he placed a coaster on it and went into the men's room. Above the toilet was a window. Saul stood on the seat and pried the window open, slipping through it and onto a loading dock.

After another half an hour of walking and maneuvering, Saul decided to pay Tentorio a visit. The sunlight was ripening so he knew the confessions would begin soon. It was best to arrive beforehand, and when he did, an altar boy approached him.

"I'm standing in for Father Roberts," he said. "I'm to tell parishioners that they may help themselves to coffee or tea while they wait for confession."

"Thanks, kid, but I'm here to see Father Tentorio about a personal matter. Do me a favor and fetch him."

The toe-haired kid flushed at the cheek. "I don't think I can do that, mister," he began, looking behind him for help or answers or perhaps just to avoid Saul's penetrating stare.

Saul bent over and said, "Sure you can, kid. Just walk back into that rectory there and tell him Saul's come by."

"I have to stand here, mister. I got my orders."

"Look, kid, I'll tell all the old folks that they should fix their drinks. Hell, I'll even pour the drinks for them. Tentorio will get sore with you if you neglect to fetch him."

The altar boy twisted his hands into knots, chewed on his lip, and then agreed. He turned around and Saul said, "And kid—"

The boy turned around.

"Don't do that with your hands. Makes you look weak."

The boy ran off.

A few older couples came into the church and Saul stayed true to his word. He explained that Tentorio was going to be delayed and that they should help themselves to the amenities that the church had provided. For one woman, he poured a coffee, added two sugars, and stirred for her as her hands were riddled with shake.

Saul didn't see the priest walk up, but heard the others greet him with reverence. Saul hadn't considered the idea that Tentorio was a respected man. He merely saw the priest as a man at a bar, a man who helped him. Perhaps, he considered as he watched the priest interact with his flock, the closest thing he had to a friend. As if he'd heard Saul's thoughts, Tentorio came over and greeted him.

"Hello, friend!"

"Sorry to pull you away from your preparations, Father."

"Nonsense. I imagine you have something you want to share. I'm eager to hear what you've discovered about our little mystery."

Something was off. Tentorio's voice sounded, warbled. Not like his own.

Saul said, "I imagine I should follow the same rules as last time."

"Rules?"

"The last time I came here, I had to take Communion."

"Of course!"

Another priest approached them. "Saul," he said.

"I was just about to bring him to you, Father Tentorio."

"Thank you, Father Jonathan."

"The hell you were," Saul said.

"Pardon?" Jonathan said.

"The hell you were going to bring me to him."

"Saul, what are you talking about?" Tentorio said.

"I've upset him somehow. I'll leave you be," Jonathan said and left. When he'd passed the pulpit, he gave a furtive glance and then disappeared into the back.

Saul kept his attention trained on the door and said, "I don't trust him."

"Why not?"

Saul thought to tell him that Jonathan had tried to pass himself off as Tentorio but it wouldn't make sense to him. Saul couldn't even make sense of his trouble distinguishing people. It's something that seemed to grow worse as he met more.

"Call it a hunch."

"He's a good man."

"I don't see it that way, Father."

Tentorio looked to the grand rose window in the west of the building. "It's a wondrous thing to see when there's sun."

"I'm sorry, what?"

"The window. It's a grand thing to see when the sun comes through it. Christ on the cross. The greatest gift. But there's scarcely sun anymore. These are dark times, friend." Tentorio shook his head and turned around to see parishioners gathering in the hall. He took a few steps in their direction and said, "Does anyone object to me hearing this man's confessions first?"

No one objected. Rather, they warm-heartedly encouraged the priest to hear Saul's confessions first. "He is a good man," one of the older women said.

Walking toward the confessional booth, Tentorio said, "They wouldn't think you so kind if they knew how much you scared that altar boy, Billy Mallroy."

"The kid's soft," Saul said.

"They're altar boys, Saul, they're not supposed to be tough."

Approaching the confessional booth, Saul stopped Tentorio and said, "What did you mean back there—dark times?"

"Sometimes, Saul, I wonder if Christ could've possibly seen the evil man is capable of. Why should you trust any man in this these times?"

"I trust you, Father. As far as I'm able to trust a man."

They entered the booth and Saul said, "I'd like to begin with a confession."

"You're humoring me, but I'll bite. What is it, my son?"

"I find my friend to be a pain in the ass."

Tentorio laughed and said, "I have the same problem." He opened something on the other side of the mesh, then moved a piece of fabric.

Saul attempted to figure out what the sounds were. He guessed a Bible and some sort of holy garment, but found himself imagining an elaborate recording device, that, once unfolded, transcribed sound into notes by way of a thin-line mechanical arm. He sought comfort by resting his hand on the grip of his gun.

Tentorio said, "Would you like to begin with reconciliation?"

Saul thought on it and said, "I was mean to a kid."

Tentorio said, "We must be kind to our children, son, for they are the innocents."

Saul said nothing.

"Now, Saul, what do you have to tell me?"

"I went to the building with the angel engraving."

"What engraving?"

"I thought Father Jonathan would've told you. He mentioned an engraving that looks like the angel on the card."

"He didn't but I'm sure he'd have told me if he thought it was a solid lead."

"It turned out to be."

"Is that so?"

"I had my doubts, but I walked around and found an entrance in the alley with a lock that reads security cards like the one I found. There was some kind of, I don't know, lab in there."

"A lab?"

"Maybe, or surgery ward or something. Beds lined up with people sleeping. A back room with doctors and large soaking tubs. Father, one of the men in the tub sat up in a panic. He was dripping in some kind of clear jelly."

"Jelly, like you'd eat?"

"No, Something medicinal. Membranous, practically. I don't know. He had wires attached to him. Leading to some kind of monitors."

"What was he doing in the tub?"

"Hell if I know. When he sat up, someone saw me. A German man."

"How did you know he was German?"

"I heard his voice when he yelled at me to stop. Some men chased me and I hid out. I gave the slip, but still—" Saul paused, a thought caught inside him.

"Still?"

"I can't help but feel I'm being tailed. It seemed best to come here rather than go back to Merav's place."

"The church has long been a safe haven. I'm glad you came, Saul." Tentorio tapped a finger somewhere inside the booth. "What do you think this all means?"

"I think it means that Uriah and Merav were telling the truth. At least part of the truth. There's still something off and I can't quite tell what that is yet."

"Do you plan to go back there?"

"Not yet. I want to meet with Uriah. See if I can't get some backup. He has people and I'm not about to go into that place alone again."

Outside an old woman coughed and Tentorio said, "I need to attend to my parishioners now. Apologize to the boy and I will say a prayer for you so that God will absolve you of your sin. Give thanks to the Lord for He is good."

Without understanding why, Saul replied, "For His mercy endures forever." He ducked out of the booth to find a long line of parishioners awaiting reconciliation. At the end of the line, a man studied him. His gaze seemed to cut into Saul's skin. An elderly woman touched the stranger's arm and asked him a question. As the tail watched her, Saul exited through the door to which Jonathan vanished earlier. There, he ran into the boy he'd seen in the foyer.

Saul found Mallroy lingering in the backroom, likely hiding from him. "Hey, kid."

"Sir?"

"I told the priest I'd tell you sorry for giving you the spook earlier."

"I wasn't scared."

Saul pulled his coat back. The boy saw the gun in his beltline.

"Maybe a little."

"Then I'm sorry, kid." Saul gave the boy a quick smile and then walked to the back of the church where he found a windowless hallway. With his back against the wall, he moved into the rectory. An aging Deacon approached, and Saul put his finger to his lips and exited through a side door.

In the alley, a pigeon with tattered wings bathed in a puddle. It dipped its marbled feathers into the brown water, cooed, shook its head. Saul felt something he'd not remembered feeling before. A pinprick in his chest. Almost compelled to stop and touch the thing, he found himself slowing. A door opened and another Brother from the Rectory stepped out for a smoke, so Saul left. The rain began again. Slight but persistent. The last of the daylight vanished from the sky and the street lights switched on.

30

DAVID STARED hard at the old woman, who turned around and faced the confessional booth. When she stepped into it, David unfastened the button to his knife sheath. The blade eased from its case with little resistance. Releasing it, the handle weighed it back into its seat. There were no parishioners behind him, a happenstance that he found particularly fortuitous.

In the back room, several altar boys roughhoused. A tall blond held a shoe just out of the reach of a shorter redheaded boy. The blond passed it to another with black hair and freckles. The redhead leaping hopelessly in the air to intercept. A young priest entered the room. There were words exchanged. He led the blond away by the collar, the others followed, heads lowered.

The old woman stepped out of the confessional and back into the aisle, nearly falling, placing her hand on a pew to steady herself. She examined David for several moments, scanning him. First, along his legs, resting on the bulge of his knife, then his face.

"May God have mercy on you," she said. Her finger shaking slightly as she pointed. The finger didn't quite extend fully. A crow's hallux.

If he'd a voice, he'd have said, "I am God's assassin." Instead, he put his finger to his lips and gave a silent *hush*. She passed him and he made his way forward, opening the door.

The confessional booth was smaller than he'd imagined. A right angle seat, enough room for knees, a small ledge below a screen. An opening the height of a coffee mug, allowed David to see the priest's hands.

"Welcome, son. How long has it been since your last confession?"

The blade came free as easily as before.

"Take your time."

David rolled the handle in his palm, its wooden grip warm and smooth.

"Is this your first confession?"

The knife blade caught the light, in a hem along the cool bend in the steel. David's face reflected back at him. He aimed the light at the screen, toward the priest's face.

"Son, you toying with something?"

The sound of the priest's breath filled the booth. It was as if David wasn't breathing at all, but he knew that he was. He could feel it. He took a better hold of the knife handle. Turned his knuckles to the ground.

"There may be people waiting for their confession, son. I don't want to rush you, but the day is running short." The priest was unable to finish the word *short* before David had moved in on him.

The force of his plunge surprised David. The blade, although nicking a rib, made its way to the tender-most part of the priest's body. The older man struggled, his hands trying desperately to keep David from striking again, but it was for naught. The gore had slackened the skin, letting David pull back and stab again. The second jab brought from the priest, a small breath of air, a noise so quiet David nearly missed it himself. The corpse slumped into its seat, the head listing back at an unnatural angle.

David leaned in, slipping his other hand beneath the divider. Using the priest's jacket, he wiped the knife clean, then cracked open the door, cheek against it to spy the church. In the distance, an altar boy began prepping the pulpit for the evening's mass. Opening the door, David withdrew himself from the booth. His heels clicked against the marble floor and the sound seemed to grow louder as it traveled through the lofty building. At the entrance, rested a marble stand with a metallic bowl brimming with holy water. He slipped his hands into it and watched as the blood rose like smoke from his fingers. He thought about the majesty of the word *blood.*

As he left the church, he heard the first scream. This pleased him. It was a rare treat to witness the reaction of his work. He corrected himself as not to be lost in the pleasure of it. To avoid the distraction of earthly pleasures that would derail him from his objective.

It had started to rain while David was inside. He buttoned his coat and pulled his collar up around his neck. Taking the alleys to utilize the cover of the tall buildings and fire escapes, David hurried back to Mr. Erelim's.

23

HE'D BEEN trailing two men through the city. They looked nearly identical to him, but each had different personalities. This was obvious in their approaches to nearly everything, save for their logic. It seemed the man who pursued the lead anticipated his every move and to that David anticipated the tail's every move. A centipede of shadows, they crept through the streets until the men divided at a church. David took refuge between two shops across the street. One a delicatessen, the other a launderette.

The smell of meats and chemicals meshed in the air around him, rousing and dispelling his hunger as the wind shifted. The bricks dripped, the gray sky barely reflecting in the water. Moss, green and brown and red, ran a chaotic marque in the receding mortar. A roach darted up the wall, stopping midway. Its antennae twisted, rose, sank. The back split, aired. He'd flattened one once. Against the toe of his shoe and a concrete embankment. Pressed hard. The thing didn't die. Escaped when David had lifted his foot. A prehistoric horseman surviving off waste to spread disease. More noble than the fly. That harbinger of decay. Infecting the living and dead with their young.

He felt them, then—the thought having brought about the parturition. David began writhing against the wall, allowing the dulled edges of brickwork to clear the young free from him. Few people, if any, noticed his sciamachy. They passed without a word. One man stopped, his hands parted as if to help, and upon seeing there was nothing crawling on him, waved dismissively and carried on. Had the man not stopped, David may have missed one of his two targets leaving the cathedral, alone. The man shook something from his hands and vanished into the foot traffic.

Don't follow, a voice whispered. Whether it was a good voice or not, David couldn't say, but believed it safer to stay in the shadow of the church's lofty spires than to chase down a man who very well may have already murdered the David Iosif had seen in his second sight.

An altar boy emerged from the church, his face red and swollen. He blew a whistle and a crowd began to gather at the steps. David's mark emerged from the alley and spoke to a young man in shirtsleeves. After the mark walked away, the young man proffered a comb from his back pocket and ran it through his slick hair. Ducking into the church, the David vanished for several minutes, minutes that elongated, that multiplied and slithered into hisses and whispers. "Don't listen," he said. "They're not real." Then, a good time after entering, the mark burst out and David followed, his feet slapping against the wet pavement, shattering the puddles that pulsed with raindrops. To his surprise, the mark was less agile than he was. Each block they passed, the mark grew slower until he reached the park, where he collapsed upon a grassy knoll, unaware of David's presence.

He hid below a canopy of trees and watched the man heave, staring at the sky as if expecting it to suck him from the ground and cast him into the ether. The patter of rain worked inside David's ears in a long, dull stab. From that tapping arose the weakened voice of a small girl. *Listen,* she said. It was clear enough that David checked for people around him, but found nothing but trees and ivy. *Listen,* she said again. He crouched down and put his ear against the tree, finding the bole silent. Another voice raised then, a male, *They are all around you, streaming in torrents.* He pulled back to find the tree alive with flies. David stepped away, a twig snapping beneath his weight. The man on the grass looked to him. David didn't stir, only closed his eyes as if to disappear into the trees and hoped the night camouflaged him.

18

SAUL EMERGED on the south side of the church. A young man with his hair combed into a duck tail came running around the southeast corner, nearly knocking into Saul.

"What's the rush, kid?"

"Man's been found dead," the kid said, checking his hair with the palm of his hand.

"Where?"

"In the church. Some old-timer said it was a priest."

Saul hurried to the front of the building, where a crowd had gathered. Many spoke in hushed tones but Saul heard one of the women say, "Poor Tentorio." There was no way through the growing mass of onlookers, so he doubled back and made his way to the alley, where the Brother's cigarette still lay smoking on the fractured concrete. Saul entered the rectory and navigated his way back into the church. A few priests stood around Tentorio's body, which lay halfway out of the confessional, akimbo and bleeding.

A patrolman entered the church, removed his hat, and made the sign of the cross on his forehead. Above him, an image of Mary holding the baby Jesus altered the light streaming in from the streetlamps so the entire foyer was awash with color. An altar boy led the cop to the scene and he began asking questions.

"This is how you found him?"

"We didn't find him. Mrs. Fitzsimmons did," a short doe-haired priest said, pointing to an elderly woman who sat in a pew crying, a deacon holding her hand and cooing.

"Did she find him like this?"

"We moved him."

"Why would you move him? Never move a body."

"We didn't think he was dead," the eldest priest said, "and he's not a body. He's Father Tentorio. A beloved priest in this parish."

"I know who he is," the cop said. "The detective is going to complain when he gets here."

"Should we move him back?"

"No. Leave him here." The patrolman turned and walked over to the crying woman. When he arrived at the pew, he bent his knee and crossed his forehead. Sliding in beside her, he began to ask her questions. She shook her head and often looked to the large cross at the far end of the church. The body of Christ bowed away from the crucifix, his wrists and feet pegged. Thin and crudely cut, the body collected shadows in the nadirs of ribs, the recesses of hips, and the funnels of eyes. A specter turned wood to hang about in a static moan. Blood forever threatening to fall free of the serpentine gash in his side.

Outside the church, the crowd was beginning to surge. The further the word spread, the more people came to witness the spectacle: the loss of a beloved priest to a senseless act of violence. But was it senseless? No one knew of the surreptitious crusade lurking in the city. It wasn't in their best interest to know. And would they know which side was good? Saul was buried to his hips in it and couldn't quite understand what was happening. As best he could see, it was a war of grays.

Several uniformed officers joined the crowd and began pushing them away from the church doors. One of the cops opened the door for two detectives in plain clothes. They strolled down the aisle formed by onlookers. The first went to the body, the latter to the woman crying.

The detective inspecting the body was a slight man with fading red hair. He asked if someone had moved the body. He snapped at the priests for moving it. Pulling the door back from the booth, he looked in, bent around, craned his neck, touched the mesh. The priests moved around him, attempting to see what he saw, attempting to make sense of the murder. One priest stood apart, leaning against the back of the booth, chewing his lip.

Behind the confessional was a hallway lined with copper engravings of the Stations of the Cross. Saul snuck around and appeared on the opposite side of the confessional booth.

"What happened?" he said.

The short priest gave a small start and said, "Saul, you shouldn't be here."

He hadn't known it was Jonathan. Part of him felt relief that it was. The other part tingled with a sense of caution. "What happened?"

"It's a crime scene, Saul."

Saul leaned in closer. "What happened?"

"Someone stabbed Father Tentorio." The priest closed his eyes in a way that seemed rehearsed.

"You don't seem real broken up about it."

"Father Tentorio was my closest friend, Saul. You can't sit in judgment of how another man mourns."

"My apologies," Saul offered, looking towards the woman sitting in the pews.

Blood soaked through Tentorio's shirt forming a thin puddle on the surface against the black fabric. It was barely distinguishable. Had they not turned on the extra lights in the room, Saul wouldn't have seen it ghosting the surface. He wanted to bend down, to close Tentorio's eyelids, to end the stare of terror trapped in his lifeless expression.

"Did anyone see the guy?"

Jonathan looked over to the pews. "Mrs. Fitzsimmons got a look at him. Poor lady. To see this kind of thing." He turned to Saul and said, "Who would do such a thing?"

Saul thought about it. He knew that he'd not lost the guy tailing him, led him directly to Tentorio. He should have faced him. Put a bullet in his head. There was no choice to it now. He owed it to Tentorio.

"Did you talk to her? Do you know what he looked like?"

"Why, Saul? Are you going to take matters into your hands? You need to leave it all alone. Let the police handle it."

"Sure," Saul said backing into the dark hallway. The corridor led nearly to the back wall, but Saul had to cut south toward the pulpit to reach the door. As he did so, he heard a cry.

"You. Murderer."

Saul turned to find the woman standing. Pointing at him. Her finger wavered in the air as if held by a thin elastic band. The detective stood and attempted to remove a gun from his holster, but was hindered when Mrs. Fitzsimmons grabbed hold of his arm to urge him to pursue Saul, who skated out the back and into the alleyway. One blue suit was looking into a garbage can when Saul emerged. By the time the cop looked up, Saul was gone.

The streets blurred by and he didn't yield until there was enough distance between he and Tentorio's body that he felt safe enough to stop. Careening into the park and collapsing into the forest, Saul heaved for air. It took a long time for him to regain his breath, as if his running had exhausted all the oxygen on Earth and he and everyone wandering the streets were doomed to suck and suck until their hearts ran cold with death. The sky was much closer than Saul had ever seen it. The city buildings in the distance snagging parts of it, concealing their tips from the world below. Perhaps it would fall upon them all. Blind them and starve the land. They could wander until they began to hunt one another. Until even that was exhausted and they faded into nothing.

Something moved in the distance. Saul sat up, tried to manage the dark from his vantage point. It wouldn't be long before every cop in town was looking for him. At least they'd be looking for the hit man as well. He'd have to find the killer before they did.

His tongue was papery. His legs trembling. If he'd a memory of his life before the hotel, he'd know exactly how long it had been since he ran such a distance? He imagined it had been a long time. Saul emerged near the city square and stepped into The Wilted Tulip, where he bellied up and ordered two bottles of water and a pear tart. The woman behind the counter hammered the sale into the cash register. When Saul handed her a few bills, the drawer flew open with a ding and the waitress dished out some silver coins. Saul left them in a tip jar beside the register. Before the woman stepped away from him, he had already downed most of the first bottle of water and eaten his tart. She gathered the dish and he left, sipping at the second bottle as he went. The threat of rain kept the tourists at bay and only buskers, madmen, and locals populated the square.

30

Erelim sat in his usual place, darkness seeming to breed around him. The metal frames of low back leather chairs caught the reflection from what little light that came in through the windows. At times, the luminescence was a starry eel slithering in the air. David took a seat and as soon as he did, an arm came from the shadows and provided him with a drink. It was as if the servants were so bored that they jumped at the chance to serve, or, it occurred to him in a cold realization, that Mr. Erelim knew that David would arrive when he did. He opened his pad and wrote on it.

Saul made his way to the facility. Followed him once he left. He made several attempts to lose me. Eventually, he went to the Cathedral on South Street. I was able to hear him give a confession to a priest there. He is telling people and becoming a greater liability. I lost him after handling the priest.

"You killed the priest?"

Yes.

Erelim rubbed his chin and gave a sigh. "I suppose," he began again, "we must lose some good men in our pursuits to succeed in God's work." Erelim bowed his head. Pulled his palms together. Pointed the fingers skyward. He spoke a few words in a language David didn't understand. The old man began to quiver, then shake. Just as he was about to career off the chair, his body went rigid and right. He opened his eyes and said, "God has a plan, David. I want you to follow Saul. He will lead you to Uriah. You are to kill the old man."

David was about to stand when one of Mr. Erelim's men came into the room. The man bent down and whispered something in Mr. Erelim's ear. David watched the man's arms, how the strange ink scarred into him seemed to change with every movement. What would it feel like to have the needle dragged over his skin slowly? It was the commitment that appealed to him. The dedication to the Council. Only servants had the tattoos. They did not rise through the ranks. Their only duty was to serve. He wondered where they had come from. But understood that the Lord worked in mysterious ways. Perhaps their creation was as much a mystery as was his own.

When the servant left, Mr. Erelim said, "We have a visitor."

A priest walked into the room. Mr. Erelim motioned to an area to the right of him and a chair slid from the dark. The priest sat down, his fingers needling the ridges of an umbrella he held in his hands.

"Who are you?"

"My name is Alexander Jonathan. I am a priest at the Holy Trinity. I came to warn you that a man named Saul is looking for you." Father Jonathan motioned to David. "He knows you killed Father Tentorio."

"And why are you telling us this?" Mr. Erelim said. "Were you not friends with Father Tentorio?"

"There are missions greater than that of corporal friendship.

I've studied the Council for years. When Saul showed me his card, I began keeping tabs on him. He's dangerous."

"How did you find me?"

"An altar boy followed him," Jonathan said, pointing to David. "Said he looked suspicious. I told him I'd check into it. To leave the cops out of it until I confirmed that it was a solid lead."

"An altar boy?" Erelim said his eyes cutting to David.

"Yes."

"Are you planning on telling the police?"

"No."

"And what do you hope to get out of this, Father Jonathan?"

Jonathan licked his already moist lips, the crinkle of thick saliva filling the room, "I'm hoping the Council will allow me to serve."

With blank face Erelim said, "Father Jonathan, we recruit our members and have never before accepted a member who approached us. However, I can speak to someone on your behalf. These matters are not mine. You must understand that we have our independent orders and responsibilities. I cannot make promises."

"I understand."

"David, you may leave. Do not disappoint me."

David looked at Jonathan.

"I will be fine, David," Erelim said. "Go on."

David walked to the window. Why they always used the window was a mystery to him still. However, he figured the old man had his reasons. He ducked through and descended the rusting fire escape onto the blackened streets.

18

OUTSIDE, THE rain began again. Slight but persistent. The moon was barely visible behind the pillows of clouds. Overhead, the lights caught the drizzle in a slow-motion light show. Saul pulled his photo out and looked at the face. Tried to memorize some aspect of it so that he could identify the man who killed Tentorio. Across the street, he saw a man sheltering beneath discarded drywall. He could feel the guy's eyes on him, so Saul walked in the company of shadows. When the man crossed the street, Saul slowed his pace to allow him to get a little closer drawing his gun close to his side.

Saul stepped inside a recessed storefront and waited. From the sidewalk, the lopsided steps of the tramp grew louder, and when he passed the entrance, Saul grabbed him. The homeless man struggled against his hold, but Saul pressed him still against a plane of thick glass.

"Who are you?"

The man struggled to get his words out, but Saul's forearm made getting them beyond his throat difficult. "David," he managed.

Saul pressed harder, almost too hard. "You've been sent to kill me?"

David shook his head as best he could. Saul pulled a photo from his pocket, held it next to David's head.

"Bullshit," he said.

"Please," David said, "I'll explain."

Saul removed his gun. Placed the barrel snug against the soft bed of flesh beneath David's chin. The pallid skin puckered. The mylohyoid muscle resisting.

David took as deep a breath as the gun allowed and began, "I started following you in the alley. After you hid. I need to warn you."

Saul pressed harder against the man's throat, choking him again.

"You killed Tentorio."

David shook his head. "I know who did." He hissed against the pressure on his neck. "He was sent by a man with white hair. Erelim, he's killing people. He wants us both dead. He wants all of us dead." David turned to his left, as if listening to someone. He shook his head and said, "He doesn't know about them."

Saul looked expecting to see someone, but there was nothing. His finger itched to pull the trigger. "What are you talking about?"

"Nothing. Nothing."

Saul leaned into him.

"A circus. A prophet, told me to find you. I want to show you where Erelim is."

Saul pulled the gun away, smacked David on the head with the butt and returned it beneath the chin.

"What prophet?"

"I told you," David said, his eyes rolled back. "A circus on the outskirts of town. Gypsies. Guy in a wheelchair. He's deformed. A gimp. It's not the important part. Erelim wants to kill you. I can show you where he lives."

Saul pulled the gun back and stared at the half-starved vagrant. He had bloody rags wrapped around an arm wound. Could barely keep his thoughts inside his skull. Saul grabbed him by the collar. The clothes were wrong. The guy following him had a clean suit.

23

THEY TRAVELED through the neighborhood, each street seemingly darker than the previous. The voices had grown unbearable. Everything spoke to him. Waste bins, lamps, discarded papers, the man's gun. *Break away*, they said. *Run*. The barrel of the gun was lodged between his ribs. At one point he felt the skin part its tender lips, swallow the steel. The gun fell to curling pieces. The tiny mouths digging into him.

"They're not real," he said.

A hammer to his head turned his vision white.

"Shut up," the man said. His breath against David's neck, warm and unfriendly.

They arrived at a residential block. A lone diner sat at the far end, its open sign glowing in the window. One street lamp held a spot of light on the ground, but the night seemed to encroach on everything else.

"Stop here."

David obeyed. The hand on his back guided him into a hallway. They climbed the staircase. At first, David attempted to count the steps, a distraction he sometimes found helpful when hearing voices. However, the more he tried to drown them out, the more persistent they seemed to be. At the first landing, he paused. A banister decoration shaped like a lion's head opened its mouth.

He's taking you to your death.

"I can't run," David said, "he'll shoot me."

"Who are you talking to?"

David felt the man's hand grab him, force him against the wall, frisk him.

"Are you wearing a device?"

"A device?"

"Some kind of ham radio."

"No," David said. "I was talking to the—" He paused and changed the direction of his excuse. "I hear things. Sometimes I don't know what's real."

The man flipped him around. Put the gun in his face.

"David, listen."

Pushing the gun deeper, Saul said, "My name is Saul."

"No, it's David. We're all David," David stuttered.

"I'm not one of you."

"Of course you are."

"No."

"Do you have a flaw?"

"What?"

"A flaw. All Davids have a flaw."

Saul seemed to consider this and said, "Your flaw is madness?"

"Something like that. Visions and voices."

"I'm fine," Saul said.

A voice came from the shadows. One of the new voices. Soft and decidedly female. It started in one corner of the hall and moved towards him. *Why doesn't he recognize you are twins?*

David repeated the question.

Saul thought on it and finally said, "I'm not David."

David opened his mouth to speak, but Saul moved the gun into it. David stopped pressing the issue. Attempted to smile.

"No, you're not," he managed around the steel.

"Keep moving," Saul said, and pushed him up the steps.

The uncomfortable knot of fist and cloth pinched the tender flesh between David's shoulder blades. He thought of his skin coming asunder. The rip. The rain of parasites fleeing him.

"I hope they feed on you," David said.

"I don't care what you're talking about. Next thing you say to me, I'm putting a bullet in you."

David bit against his lip. He focused on his breath. In. Out. Something about being with Saul exacerbated the voices, made them more present than they'd ever been. In. Out. Saul navigated him onto a landing and into a somber hall. In. Out. From below a door, a blade of light cut the dark. In. Out. He was stopped. Saul removed a key, unlocked the door. They entered. In.

The woman he'd seen at the cafe stood in the living room, her hair blond, the bangs sharp above the eyebrows. She stubbed a cigarette into a silver ashtray. Her gray skirt billowed as she walked, tugging on the cuffs of her white blouse for good measure.

"Who is this?" she said as she carved along David's jaw with the pad of her index finger.

Saul led David to the center of the room and pushed him into a chair. The voices hissed around him. A din of unearthly calls to run, to attack, to fall upon the ground with his hands over his head, to bite the flesh from his wrists. He tried to summon Ileana's calming voice, but the others were too loud.

18

THEY SAT and stared at one another. Merav taking a few longer looks at Saul than at David. Her face in Saul's peripheral vision, distorted and angry. This annoyed him. On the couch, David twitched, rubbed his thighs, spoke occasionally. Hushed reassurances to himself.

"David," Saul asked, his voice a violent break in the silence, "what was that you said in the stairs? The thing about all the Davids."

Merav's head made a sharp jerk toward Saul, her eyelids opening and then sliding back to their natural slits.

"I didn't, I said it was nothing." He worked at his hands.

"I won't hit you, David. Just tell me what you said in the hall."

Merav reached for a cigarette and said, "This is a waste of time, Saul."

"David, go ahead." Saul hid the gun behind his back.

"You woke up like me. Right? A hotel. A note. We're the same. It's what I was getting at. The man with the silver hair, Erelim. He's involved."

Merav exhaled a breath of smoke. "Of course he says that,

Saul." She stood and approached David. "We've taken great precautions to let everyone think you're one of them."

Merav palmed David's neck and he flinched.

"They said I shouldn't be seen by her or the old man."

"Who said that?" Merav asked.

"A prophet at a circus," Saul said.

"Oh, a prophet," Merav laughed, "this *does* sound important."

She sat back down, paying close attention to the burning paper in her hand. Watching it as the smoke snaked from its ember. Saul waited for her to speak again, but she did not.

"He knows where Erelim is."

"I'd like to leave," David said.

Saul recognized the fear in David's eyes. Round and wild like there was some animal inside scratching to get out. Merav seemed not to understand, or care. She fingered her armrest, lost in some thought or another. There was, Saul admitted to himself, something off about it. Again, he found himself wondering what to trust.

Merav stood and traipsed toward the bar. She pulled out three glasses, poured drinks, and brought them back to the sitting area. When handed his, David stared at it, apprehension fingering his brow. She shook her head and took it from him, sipped, and said, "See, no drugs." She handed Saul his and said, "You, however, shouldn't be so sure." Taking her seat, Merav continued, "We have to see Mr. Uriah. He'll tell us what to do." She placed her glass on the table and continued, "There's no sense in lingering around here." Saul looked into his drink, shaking thin waves along the curves of crystal as she walked into a side hall. Soon the room ticked with the whirl of a phone's rotary dial.

"Saul, Iosif told me not to let the woman or old man see me. Please. I want to leave now."

Saul didn't answer. Sucked at something in his tooth. Sipped his drink.

"They're going to kill me."

"Are you a spy?"

"What?"

"I said, are you a spy?"

"No."

"Then, I won't let them kill you."

This answer seemed to satisfy David as he finished his drink and sat calmly with his hands in his lap. Saul collected the empty crystal and put it back atop the bar. Things were going to change soon. He wasn't sure how but he could feel the future in his bones. He checked the clip to make sure he was fully loaded. Saul's body loosened, the gin quick on his empty stomach.

Merav returned from the hallway with a different hair color—black. It occurred to Saul that she must keep hairpieces in different parts of her home. He thought of the reasoning behind why someone would change wigs so frequently, but understood that much of the world was not as it seemed.

She packed a small clutch bag with her cigarette case, a lighter, and a pearl penknife. When she fastened the clasp, she inspected herself in the mirror, arching the left eyebrow slightly. With a sigh, that seemed more authentic than anything she'd ever spoken, she walked into the bedroom. David, curiosity fingering a ripple of flesh in the center of his forehead, looked at Saul. Before either could speak, Merav returned with a pair of slacks, a clean shirt, and a jacket.

"You need to shower and change. There are medical supplies in the medicine cabinet. Clean and wrap your arm."

David took the clothes without pause. Merav led him to the bathroom, closed the door behind him, and returned to the living room.

"Mr. Uriah's a frail man. I don't want to track in any more germs than we have to," she said, rounding the bar and refreshing their drinks.

"He and I have to go somewhere first."

"Where?"

"An errand."

She released smoke from her mouth. It drifted to her nose like a vapor of warm milk. "Fine, but we should make it quick."

"You misunderstand. He and I are going on the errand. You're going to Mr. Uriah's and we'll meet you there."

"Saul."

"Merav, I'm not going to risk you going with us. I'll bring him with me. You've got my word."

"What are you doing?"

"I need to pay a debt. That's all."

They drank in silence. Saul examined a thin-line vein that ran along the mound of her esophagus. It was the first time he'd seen it. Somehow it made her seem more fragile. An urge to kiss her began rising in him but was cut short when David emerged, a clean rack for the suit of a larger man. David fussed at the jacket cuffs, but let down his arms as if defeated by the coat.

Without a word, Merav went to the front door and opened it. David made a motion that he would follow Saul.

"Not happening. Get in front, David. If you make one move that I don't like, I'll end you."

David did as he was told. They entered the hall and Merav joined them, bolting the door before she did. Saul pressed the nose of his gun into the small of David's back. With a slight nudge, he told David to lead the way. He moved through the gloom with great difficulty, laboring under the new cloths as if they outweighed him. At one point, he slowed and Saul pressed the gun deeper. A dim light marked the stairs before them. David rounded the corner and grabbed the banister to steady himself.

30

THE NIGHT suffocated the city. Even those crepuscular creatures, which often stirred in the alleys and among the gutters, were choked of noise. Occasionally a car in some other part of the neighborhood would awaken and lumber off, its engine rattling and kicking. The moon, if it still existed, was swallowed whole by a low ceiling of clouds. David approached the front of the building and looked up. The light was off. With his gun pulled, he entered and approached the staircase. Somewhere in the coiling structure of steps, voices echoed.

"Just keep moving."

There were three different sets of feet. A dull set, a new set of male shoes, and a woman's heels. David slipped his shoes off and set them to the side of the stairwell. The marble cold against his feet, he ascended. Examining the curve of the wall, he studied the shadows. Large at first, the shadow, humpbacked and awkward, began to shrink. The people crept forward, close together as if stitched. He checked his safety. When he reached the second level, he perched his elbow on the rail. Watched the wall.

The shadow grew so small and trembling that David knew they'd round the corner at any moment, he raised and leveled his piece, angled it favoring his left, only slightly. Then, as if a mist, two bodies emerged from around the bend. One stopped and the other tried to push him. The angle wasn't quite right. He'd not expect three in his calculation. Had to be sure about hitting the right ones. David backed away and descended. He gathered his shoes and left the building.

Across the street, a lamp flicked at the entrance of the park. Each flicker grew darker until the bulb went dead. David hurried across the street and took refuge in the shadows between maples. He could feel his breath as it swelled in his chest and pushed between his lips.

Three people emerged from the building. Saul, David, and Merav.

Merav said, "Why didn't you shoot him?"

"I didn't see him."

Merav asked the other David if this was true but he refused to answer or answered so quietly that David couldn't hear him from his vantage point. He wanted more than anything to shoot them but needed them to lead him to Uriah.

Merav pointed to the park. Almost directly at him. David pulled his gun free, leveled it. However, it became clear that she'd not seen him. She pointed another way. Merav walked to the left and the men to the right. Although Mr. Erelim had suggested he tail Saul, it stood to reason that the woman would be his best avenue to find Uriah. Before he'd weighed the options fully, he found himself tracking her.

The rainstorms had washed the streets of tourists. Only commuters and the occasional socialite wandered the streets. This made it difficult for David to tail closely. He couldn't shake the fear of losing her, but understood she would catch him if he pushed it and crept closer. They passed a dancehall where big band music pulsed through the open doors, the horns ricocheting against buildings across the way. On the corner, a band of traveling men played Gypsy folk music and a few drunk tourists danced around them. One of the traveling men stepped away from the musicians. He fingered an accordion, his waxed mustache unmoved by the hiss and suck of the instrument, and began to sing a love song about a woman with a heart made of vines and hands made of silver. There was nothing to the moment that allured David. The closeness of dance and the unshapely sound of music. They were not God's plan. They were earthly distractions. The language of God was not musical. It was utilitarian. Before Adam was exiled from Eden, he named those things that were his dominion. It was after that he was forced to create supplementary language. Words to describe, to transition, to negate. He, in his misery, wished to create a garden of air, replace those blooms of paradise with language. This was what became of it. City streets lined with litter and vermin. Bricked walkways ushering men and women into shops and bistros, theaters and brick-faced apartments.

18

A CONGRESS of shadows gathered in the alley. Perhaps they'd gathered to decide Saul's fate. Certainly it seemed much darker than it truly was, as it was the blackest corner of the world he'd ever seen. David plodded forward with greater caution, looking to the sky as if a cauldron of unearthly vultures might spiral upon him at any moment. Saul could hardly blame him. In this world they'd been born to, there was only mystery. Who was to say that the madman wasn't hearing voices or seeing things to which Saul was blind? That the sky couldn't open and a sea of raptors wouldn't descend upon them with talon and beak? David stopped short and pointed directly above, to a fire escape that was slightly out of reach.

"Here," he said. "This is where the old man jumped and climbed."

"The fire escape?"

"Yes."

"Why the fire escape?"

David shrugged.

"How old is this guy?"

"Older than we know."

"What the fuck does that mean?"

David picked at his fingernails. He'd not look up but said, "I think there are things older than the universe."

"Well, if there are, I don't want to know," Saul said. "Let's get up there."

"No."

"No?"

"He'll kill me."

"I'm sure he'll try to kill both of us. We're not coming to give him a housewarming present."

"What do you plan to do?"

"I plan to find the man who killed my friend and shoot him dead."

David shook his head. "You lied to the woman. I know you saw the man in the hallway. You didn't recognize him."

"No one got hurt. Now, let's go."

"You can't kill the old man."

"Why not?"

"There are some things—"

"Stop with that shit."

"I'm just saying—"

"David, does the man walk?"

"Yes."

"Does he breathe air?"

"Yes."

"Then he can die. All of them can die."

David bit on his lip, uncertain if he should reply.

"And stop with all this Heaven and Hell business. There's nothing but this rotten world and we're all doomed to die in it. If we die tonight or tomorrow, it doesn't make one bit of difference. We're going to die. Now, up."

David looked at the ladder and then back to Saul, who could see the man shivering. Anxiety locking him in place. Whether or not Erelim could be killed was not important. David believed it enough that it made it so for him. Saul edged him out of the way.

"Follow me and don't make me shoot you."

"Okay."

Saul jumped and grabbed hold of the bottom rung of the ladder. The metal was worn smooth from years of use. He climbed up several rungs before signaling for David to follow. Without knowing why, Saul sniffed his free hand, caught a snort of rust. He looked at the rung beneath his hand but saw none. Did metal rust in secret? He ascended with caution until David said to stop.

David climbed closer and whispered, "He's on the next level. He might see us climbing."

Saul pulled the gun free from his belt. It was difficult but he managed the next few steps armed.

He crawled onto the landing, turning around and signaling for David to wait just below. Peeking into the window, Saul saw very little. As he focused, he made from the dark, two shapes sitting in chairs. Try though he might, Saul could hear nothing through the open window. It was to his advantage that the alley ran perpendicular to a street with traffic. The whirring and honking disguised his approach, an issue he'd not thought through upon his ascent. The silhouette facing the window stood and left the room. Even if he wasn't leaving for the night, this would be the best time for Saul to strike.

"Don't come until I call your name. Got it?"

"Yes."

Slipping a leg over the windowsill, Saul moved through the room without so much as a sound. The man in the room was still facing the door. Saul eased closer, hoping the floorboards wouldn't moan beneath him. He slipped his left hand over the man's mouth and pushed the barrel of his gun into the man's temple.

"Make a sound and I'll pull the trigger."

The man agreed.

"I'm going to ask you a question. You answer me in a whisper. Don't look at me. Don't move."

The man's breath was short and jagged, fear controlling him.

"Where is Erelim?" Saul eased his grip and moved his hand from the mouth to the man's chin.

"He's left."

Two words were enough for Saul to recognize the voice. His instinct drove him to wrap his arm around Jonathan's neck. He pulled back against the frame of the chair. A vein was swelling in Saul's neck. The blood hammering through him. Jonathan's hands flailed about, slapping at Saul's head, awkward and weak.

"You son-of-a-bitch, you're part of this? You killed Tentorio."

Jonathan tried to shake his head but couldn't. He was fading. Saul could feel it. The consciousness about to leave him. Saul eased up. Jonathan coughed. To stifle this, Saul wrapped his hand around Jonathan's mouth, felt the priest buck against the restraint.

"Tell me what happened," Saul said and then eased his grip to allow the man to answer.

"It wasn't me, Saul. It was another man. He looks a lot like you."

"Why are you here?"

"I came to talk to them."

"You're lying."

"I'm not."

"The face gives a man up. Your right eyelid fluttered when you answered me. Just enough."

"This coming from a man with prosopagnosia."

"What?"

"You have prosopagnosia, Saul. You wouldn't know it by this name. I noticed it the night at the bar. You've noticed it, haven't you? Trouble identifying others by face. You use other clues, likely. Voices, hair, clothing. It's why you waited until I spoke just now."

"What's that got to do with anything?"

"How can you claim to know I'm lying by facial tics, if you can't even remember my face?"

It wasn't so much the comment, but the wry smile that followed which drove Saul to lift his hand in the air and bring the butt of his gun down upon the bridge of Jonathan's nose, his eye socket, his mouth. Again and again until the man stopped yelling. His hands stopped trying to protect his face. His heart stopped beating. The skull, crushed into a dark sinkhole, lilted to the side and the body slid onto the floor. Blood peppered Saul's face. His heart raced. Since waking in the hotel, it was the first time he'd felt alive, whole. It was what he was born to do, and he now understood this more than anything he'd understood before. Wiping the blood free from his gun as he walked, Saul searched the adjacent room to find it empty. They knew he was on the fire escape. They'd left Jonathan to die.

A noise came at the window. Saul turned on his heel and aimed. It was David lumbering in like some wingless bird. With greater difficulty managing the dark, he stepped through as if there were tripwires strewn over thin ice. It wasn't until he was close to stepping on the priest that he saw the blood glinting in pale streetlight, abject quartz. A gasp hitched in his throat.

"What happened? This is terrible. Terrible."

"Don't bother yourself with it," Saul said.

"You murdered him."

"Some men need to be murdered."

David put his hands over his ears. He shook his head as if loosening things inside to cast them into the dark. Saul walked to him, gently wrapped a hand around his elbow and began guiding him toward the window. When they'd emerged from the building, Saul pulled David's hands from his ears.

"I don't aim to kill you, David."

"I want to go."

"Go?"

"Leave."

"Not 'till this is all sorted. Wait on the fire escape. I need to look around."

Saul walked down a long hallway with no decorations, windows, or doors, save for one at the end. With each step it seemed the walls were growing closer to him, the doorway further away. He pushed his back against the wall so that he could look to both entryways. This managed to give him a small semblance of security. He pushed the door open with his toe. Well oiled, it swung wide without sound.

Floor to ceiling bookcases filled with books, none having a title printed upon the spines, lined the walls. There was a single metal folding chair in the center of the room, with a standing lamp to its side. Saul pulled a book from the shelf. Opened it.

The first several pages were filled with text so small that it was difficult to decipher as handwriting. He lowered the book into the lamplight, and finding no language he could understand, flipped farther into the book, where he found images drawn of faceless men, a sequence of numbers above each. 31.01 – 31.24. Removing another book, he found much the same. However, the numbers altered. 32.01 – 32.24. His stomach gave a lurch and he dropped the book onto the chair.

The rest of the rooms in the apartment matched in their lack of furnishings. There was, in fact, no bed. No items that would indicate that someone lived in the apartment at all except for the chairs and fully stocked bar. The last room he searched had been lined with burlap and several bags of grain, which had small indentations in them. Saul wondered if this was where they slept. When he'd swept the apartment completely, he joined David outside the window, where he was whispering something, but Saul could tell that David wasn't talking to him but to someone or something in the ether of his madness. Saul motioned and David began his descent. If Tentorio's killer was anything like Saul, he'd probably figured out where Uriah lived and was probably already there.

30

THE DAMP mortar seemed to catch fire beneath the lights of the thoroughfare. As David stepped over it, his heels ground against the dirty bricks. The arcade was empty, save for two drunken men sleeping next to the fountain. The Overbee came to mind.

On one of the many side streets that poured into the arcade, a young man with slicked hair and an expensive suit, attempted to open a sedan but his inebriation made the routine a chore. He shook his keys as he wavered, looked at Merav and said, "Aren't you a looker?"

It was if she knew he'd say it. She ignored him, no part of her revealing that she heard his voice at all. When David passed him, the stranger was attempting to line his key with the lock. He dipped forward, catching himself at the last moment with an elbow or knee.

The chase, David found, was lacking. Distracted by something, Merav did little to make it difficult, only occasionally looking behind her and changing direction three times. It gave him pause. Was she setting him up? If so, he'd be at the ready. He drew his gun.

When Merav entered the Overbee hotel, David waited for

a while to ensure the destination wasn't a ruse. At the end of an hour, he emerged from the shadows and searched the back alley for alternate entrances. There, a row of fire escapes, just out of arm's reach flanked the buildings. To the left of the kitchen's door was an overturned white bucket, cigarette butts scattered about. David moved the pail and placed it under the ladder. It was still short. He scanned the alley again. This time he found a burned office chair. The cushions had melted into a sling of plastic and ash. The wheels howled and hiccupped against the asphalt. At times, they surrendered completely and David had to lay a shoulder into the back to get them to snap into action. Sooty water stained his new jacket. The dull streetlamp gave a ghostlike glow in the wet blemish.

When he finally got the chair beneath the fire escape, he tilted the back on its spring. It bent with great difficulty, but David finally managed to wedge the metal frame in the gap where the mortar had receded between two bricks. He gave the chair a shake. It didn't dislodge. He placed the bucket on the seat. Wiggled it into position.

Stepping back several paces, David took a deep breath and ran. With a leap, his foot cleared the edge and made contact with the flat face of the pail's bottom. As he pushed off, the chair rolled back, collapsed to the ground, but it wouldn't matter. David felt his hand connect with the ladder. His body swung for an instant, but he was able to pull himself to the second rung and secure his weight. He climbed.

The hallway on the fifth floor was vacant, so David stepped upon the grated landing and attempted to lift the window. It jostled in its track but wouldn't open. He removed his coat, placed it over the bottom left pane of glass, and knocked the window out with the butt of his gun. Clearing the shards of lingering glass away with the jacket, he eased his left arm in and pulled the security combination lock toward him. David closed his eyes and allowed his fingers to guide him through the numbers.

The world went black. From beneath the veil of his eyelids, the slight movements of the rotating disk seemed expansive. He could feel when he'd hit the cam. As he turned to the final number and the lock came free, he thought, God is truly great. He looped the shackle out of the metal bars and swung the gate open. As it crept to the side, David opened the window and stepped inside the hallway, the glass crunching beneath his steps.

23

THE OLD man rolled his chair closer. David sat still. Mr. Uriah was more present than the feeling of blood easing through his body and the subsequent awareness of grubs sewing their tiny hooked mouths into his flesh. The wheelchair snagged on the corner of an Oriental rug. The old man fussed with the wheels but never took his gaze off David.

Merav stepped out of the shadows and pulled the chair from its snag and then vanished just as quickly as she had emerged. Mr. Uriah stretched his finger out, a bone covered loosely in flesh. As he inched it toward David's hand, his skin tingled as if it were going to retreat and leave his hands bare to the old man's touch. He imagined a nightshade, pulled and released, rocketing back to relax the tension. When the image faded away, the bony finger made contact. There was no shock. No separation of his flesh. Only a touch, like any other.

"Where are you from?" Mr. Uriah asked, the reflection of light in his glasses hiding his deep-set eyes.

"I told you who he is," Saul said.

The old man shushed Saul and said, "I want to hear it from him."

The terrible mist of his voice was all whispers inside the hole in his throat, monstrous and shallow. David looked to Saul for reassurance but found none. He cleared his throat and answered, "Hotel South."

"I see. And you say you escaped Erelim?"

"Only barely. He keeps finding me."

"How lucky for you," the old man said. "You've managed to escape certain death. How many times?" he asked, his whisper rising in pitch.

"Five times."

"You can understand how I have trouble believing that a man who thinks objects are speaking to him could possibly escape Erelim."

"I run."

"Oh! Merav, do you hear that? He runs," the old man said, the words punctuated and feeble.

"Quit taunting him," Saul said. "He took me to Erelim's place."

"So you've said. Forgive me, Saul, if I don't trust your judgment, but I worry this is a set-up."

As if on cue, there was a noise from the hall, and everyone in the room looked toward the door.

"Saul, Merav, would you mind terribly checking on that commotion?"

David said, "Please stay, Saul."

Merav stepped forward and grabbed Saul's hand. "He'll be okay here. I give you my word." She looked at the old man, "My word, Mr. Uriah."

The old man acquiesced.

Saul looked back toward David as the couple left the room. Once the clacking of their footsteps shrank and eventually vanished altogether, the room was filled with the pressing weight of silence, save the whisper of air coming through the hole in the man's throat. David wondered how big the suite was that it could lose the sound of people walking. The building consumed a city block. Hundreds of windows, yet the penthouse was surprisingly devoid of them.

When the old man grew so close that it seemed as if he might pull himself onto David's lap, he stopped and leaned forward until David could smell the bitter scent of medicine on his breath. He released a long hiss through the hole in his throat. David focused on a small worm that began emerging from that fleshy pit.

David met his stare and said, "I'd like to leave."

"We're just getting to know one another." He rolled back a few inches and pointed to a glass tube that hung above his head, the room's light shone through it like a small golden sun.

"What's in there?"

"This," he said, "is medicine that will make all the pain go away." He clicked a button and a mechanical spider crept upon his scalp. David pushed against the carpet to back away, but the effort was for naught. There was a tremor in his heart and his breath caught somewhere inside him. The device bit into the old man's scalp and his face went slack for a second before he reanimated. The apparatus sighed and retreated behind the wheelchair. Mr. Uriah's top lip rose above his small round teeth, which looked more like unpolished pearls than did they dentin. The smile faded and a strange look came over the man's face, as if someone had twisted something on the inside of him. "Now," he said, pulling a syringe from a brown leather pannier slung over his armrest, "this is for you." Before

David could run, the needle was inside him. The room began to grow fuzzy, the air lighter.

"See," the old man whispered. "The pain goes away."

"I've told you everything."

From behind him, hands tied David to his chair and he found himself unable to move to fight them off. His muscles were slack. Still, he could feel the restraints tightening, the pain of their final cinch. From beneath them, grubs began to creep out. He closed his eyes, tried to focus. They weren't there. It was as simple as that. They weren't there. Behind his eyelids he often found the cure to his own malady, if only for a brief moment. He thought of the old man with powder white hair of the cripple, of the fire dancers. He remembered the trailer he woke in and the calm of that moment, the wholeness he felt, and just as he allowed himself to be lost in that memory and the pain in his arm was beginning to subside, something emerged from that inner dark—a fervid white pain far different from any he'd felt before.

The old man removed the sharpened end of his cane from David's muscle and said, "I can bring you peace or I can bring you pain. The choice is yours."

"I told you. I'm not like them." David was interrupted by another stab.

The world went white and he brayed.

18

THERE WAS nothing in the hall. The door was closed and locked.

David began screaming.

"Was this a trick?" Saul said.

Merav looked down the hallway, her clenched jaw betraying her typical, detached distance. "No, he knows I gave my word," she said, her lips curling into an odd smile, as if she too believed they'd been had. Saul couldn't read it. Couldn't say with certainty that she was being honest.

Saul reached for his gun, but Merav eased her hand over his.

"Please," she said, "I'll go check on it. You should stay here. It's safer."

"What do you mean safer?"

"We're not alone," she whispered in his ear and then left the room the way a spirit leaves a corpse, quick and silent.

It struck him again how far this mystery seemed to reach. There were players he'd yet to see. Figures that lay about the perimeter of the baleful city. Was this, he wondered, how an ant feels when searching for food among the seemingly infinite folds of a carnation? He'd like to think the image was something from his life, a childhood memory perhaps, but found himself growing red at the realization that he could only remember his life as it began in a hotel room with a name, a number, and a question. Saul pulled the gun from his waist and armed it. If there were others, he'd shoot them, over and over until there was no ammunition, and then he'd use his hands.

He heard Merav's voice in the distance.

"I promised him."

Saul had never heard Merav raise her voice before. He advanced. The sound of his footsteps seemed inhuman. Steps of a giant. Looking around, he bent and removed his shoes. As he began moving forward, he remembered the man putting his shoes on in Merav's foyer. He'd been foolish. There was a sound at the door behind him. Something small and metallic akin to a wind-up bug scratching at wood. As the knob on the back door began to turn, Saul backed into the shadows.

A thin man in a fedora stepped past the threshold. When he was nearly into the hall, Saul looked to his feet and saw that he was shoeless. Without a word, Saul raised his gun and fired a shot.

30

THE FIRST shot came before David entered the suite. He fell to the ground, the bullet just grazing his left ear. In his fall, David squeezed a shot that did little outside of displace his opponent; however, it gave him time to stand. Saul backed into a room and David slipped into the adjoining office where he found a bar with a few glasses resting upon its top. His ear began to throb. Saul's labored breath ricocheted in the hall. He was close. David grabbed a small mirror from the wall. Kneeling, he eased it into the hall and angled it until he could see the tip of Saul's gun poking from around the corner. Leaning into his shoulder, he aimed for where he approximated Saul's shins would emerge.

"You're outmanned."

Although David knew this was probably true, he would manage it as it came. He held his aim steady.

"I know you're here."

The gun's nose vanished, and a few moments later, a mirror took its place. The two mirrors reflected one another in an infinity of futilities. David pulled back and placed his ear against the wall. As he did this, he heard Saul tapping lightly, undoubtedly testing to see if he could fire through it. Despite falling on opposite sides of the issue, the similarities

196

were remarkable. A thought that David found to evidence the progress Erelim had made with the brothers.

There were more steps in the hallway, so David held the mirror out again. This time he saw two men in black slacks walking at the far end of the hall. Soon, Saul leaned his mirror out, the papered back facing David this time. His opponent was uncertain. David took this opportunity and fired, shattering Saul's mirror.

When the henchmen stepped into the light, David saw that they looked much like Erelim's but their skin was different. Their tattoos filled in all black. They spread to opposite sides of the hallway and held their positions. Saul called out, "We can sit here all night or we can face off. Eventually one of us is going to get to you."

There was logic to this. David rose to his feet and peeked around the corner. He took a shot and leveled one of the henchmen. When this occurred, he saw a few more henchmen edge their heads out of doors farther down the hall. He leaned back into his room, checked his ammunition. He could kill four more, five if God was willing. He stepped fully into the hall and began picking men off.

One, to the head. The body dropped into a crumple. Two, in the throat. He gasped for breath as he struggled to hold the blood inside his body. Three, in the eye. He stepped back, as if shocked that the bullet could kill him. With the fourth shot, he heard a reply, but never saw the gunman. He turned to find Saul emerging from a room on the right. How had he managed to skip across the hall without David noticing? There was a brief moment of hot light. His pulse present in his ears. A gasping breath, his own. He stumbled, hit a wall, tripped on his own feet, and fell to the floor. He felt Saul's hand on his arms. Felt him turn him onto his back. Saul asked, "Did you kill Tentorio?"

David didn't reply.

"Why?" Saul said, anger rising through his voice.

David was unable to tell Saul that he'd killed the priest in the name of Christ, that Tentorio was rewarded in heaven as a sacrifice. Instead, he stared up at the ceiling, watching the edges of his world filling with the Lord's holy light. Saul slapped him.

"You're not going without telling me."

David did not.

"Speak, goddamn it."

David reached for Saul's leg and was met with a blow to the head. Then another. And another. Again and again. The pain built for a while, but soon grew dull. The sound of each blow growing wetter until the world fell silent and the room went dark. Then there was nothing.

18

SAUL ROOTED through David's pockets, finding a wooden cross and the same card that he found in his overturned room. In his breast pocket Saul found a notebook with lists of words and sentences:

Where is Smathers'?

Yes.

No.

She went into a marketplace. Foot traffic during a rainstorm.

I will stay with the woman. He will show.

The priest may be a problem, sir.

His issue: being mute. The strange reverse pump of sorrow hit Saul's heart. He would have killed the man regardless, but he'd not known. Not known he was unable to answer. This was Saul's fault. The man was unable to clear his conscience. Nor provide his motive. Saul reached out, placed his fingers on the bloodied eyes and closed, as best he could, the lids. It wasn't much, but it provided some dignity.

Saul wiped his face clear of blood spatter. There was a calm that came to him after taking a life, as if the world around him had hushed and slowed. He turned toward the bodies that lined the hallway, opaque mounds crumpled and stacked, a stream of hardwood seeming to flow between them. The wounds trickled into reflective pools, oil black in the absence of light. Two of the men's hands nearly locked, as if in their final moments, they sought comfort in the soft touch of a brother. Flipping one to his side, Saul looked for anything that might tell him who they were but his efforts came up empty. Their clothing lacked tags, their pockets laid empty. Each had a shaven head, the back of the skull inked with a language Saul didn't understand. First an upside-down *y*, an *o*, an upside down *s*. Their arms were inked black. Pulling the black undershirt of one over his bleeding head, Saul discovered another tattoo ran down the spine. Lines of text which branched from the center and grew denser as he followed them down. He removed the black wingtip shoes, slipped free the dress sock, and found the feet inked completely black, the toenails plucked free. Thinking first to re-shoe the man, Saul opted to drop the wingtip and return to his shoes.

"A grim site," Saul said, almost inaudibly, pushing the door shut before some innocent passerby could witness the scene.

Who knew how many men Uriah had hidden away in the apartment? There could be a militia of goons, blackfooted and armed, at the ready for a situation such as this. As he walked back toward Merav, two henchmen stepped from the gloom of the hallway and apprehended him. Saul struggled against them. There was a pain in his neck and the world fell dark.

23

His body filled with trembling white pain but did not come asunder, even as the old man dug his bony finger deeper and deeper into his wound. David opened his mouth, but nothing escaped. His tongue clicked at the back of his drying teeth.

"Come now," the old man whispered, "surely you must have something to tell me. Who sent you?"

David shook his head, tried to say, "No one," but nothing came out. The pain had driven language from him. The shadows in the room began to take the shape of the man-child, Iosif. His massive opaque jaw eased open, a long tongue unfurling and running around the walls. It did this three times, growing faster with every passing moment, until it moved so quickly that David could no longer follow. When the tongue stopped, it wrapped around the shadow of the old man and pulled his head free. A dry, quiet laugh banged around in David's throat. His body shook.

"Something is funny," Mr. Uriah said. He leaned forward, his finger easing into the wound he'd bored with his cane. When he hit the bone, it seemed as if electricity shot through David, a coreless vibration rattling through his muscles, branching out and bursting his nerve endings like Chinese fireworks. Just as the old man began to curl his finger and turn, Merav walked in, gasped. Mr. Uriah removed his finger and David's body went limp.

"You can't torture him."

"Of course I can, love."

"He's a lunatic, not a spy," she said, and when she could tell Mr. Uriah was unmoved, she raised her voice. "I promised him."

A bloom of stale breath eased from the hole in Mr. Uriah's neck. He curled his lips into a faint smile and said, "You did, but I did not. He's a David, and not our David. That is all I need to know." He turned and removed a mechanical reaching tool from a holster at the side of his chair. Holding it in the air, he fastened the control to his hand and hummed a childish melody. The song arose from his throat, the failing rattle of a dying snake. He wiggled his fingers and the mechanical hand mimicked his action.

"Fascinating, isn't it? I use this when my back hurts. It keeps me from leaning forward so much," Mr. Uriah said.

With all but the index finger curled into the mesh of its palm, the old man began to move it forward. Had Merav not eased her hand over the shaft and slowly pushed it away, it would have entered the wound.

Merav put her hand on Mr. Uriah's shoulder and said, "We don't have to needle him, Mr. Uriah. He'll tell us everything."

"Don't be naïve," Mr. Uriah interrupted. "He brought them upon us. There are no deviations from the design. The Davids are *all* killers."

The old man pulled a syringe from his lap and exchanged it with one from a holster hanging along his armrest. He held the needle against the light, flicking it with his finger. Small bubbles floated through the golden-green liquid.

David attempted to pull against the restraints. The world grew over with so many voices at once that he couldn't distinguish what they were saying.

"One at a time," he said.

"Of course, David. One at a time," Mr. Uriah said, sinking the needle into David's skin.

At first, there was nothing, but soon, David felt a thousand burning needles tumbling through him. The voices grew so loud, he was sure the mirrors in the room, the glasses, the syringes would all burst into pieces, but they did not. Instead, a veil of sleep overcame him.

"Quiet," he whispered just before he fell asleep. "Quiet."

18

SAUL AWOKE in a chair. On his right arm, a rope tied into a knot. On his left, the same. Across the room from him, Merav and David were asleep, bound to chairs. The two goons who'd laid hands upon Saul stood on either side of Uriah, who sat with his back to a sword that rested on the mantel of a marvelous baroque fireplace. The sparse light struck the cherubs' faces, but the shadow of their cheeks blackened their eyes. They stared at Saul, and it seemed to him that their eyes were portals to some other world. A place where secrets lived and bred.

"You're awake," Mr. Uriah said, his voice filled with an off-handed joy that Saul couldn't quite place.

Saul tried to speak, but managed only a moan.

"Go ahead, boy. You'll find your tongue again."

Clicking the muscle around in his mouth, Saul swallowed hard against the dryness. When the lump had passed down, he tried again, this time managing, "Tie," and part of, "Chair."

"Why have I tied all of you to chairs? Is that what you're asking? That's for protection, you see. After all, we had a lovely thing here until you brought along this mutt."

Saul's mouth was soft and moist once again. He motioned toward Merav and said, "You can't trust Merav? She's been devoted."

"The ways of a woman are that of deception. It has been such since she was born of Adam's rib. Besides, she'll understand when it's all said and done."

"And the ways of man? Having goons sneak around an apartment."

"Man deceives to protect. Woman deceives to gain."

One of the guards shifted, his movement causing the floorboards to moan. The light wrapped around his flesh, except in those places where he'd scarred the flesh.

Saul fussed with his binds. "Why the black arms?"

Uriah looked to one of them, reaching his hand and easing a finger along the flesh. "They are defectors. Men who once served the council. They cover their tattoos as a way to show their commitment."

"To what?"

"To me. They left with me."

Merav's head, which had drooped forward lazily, her hair abstracting her face, had begun to lull back and forth until she awoke with a panic of breath through the nose. With her mouth agape, she rolled her eyes in their sockets. She was trying to deduce. She mouthed at words the way a child gnaws at a teething ring. The reality of her predicament becoming clear to her. As she began pushing words through the haze of the sedative, Saul found a way to turn his wrist until his thumb was curling beneath his palm.

"Why?" she said.

"You know," Mr. Uriah said, his attention locked on her. The guards faced forward, into the edges of the room where light least shone.

Saul gnashed his teeth and pulled as best he could until

205

his joint was run through with pain, the rope threatened to tear his flesh, and his lungs begged to cry out. By the time he snapped the finger out of socket, it was all he could do not to howl. He eased his hand free. However, it hadn't occurred to him that he'd need his thumb to untie the other knots. With his fingertips and the ball of his palm, he fussed with one to no avail. Slipping the gimpy thumb beneath his thigh, Saul bit down upon his lip and righted the joint. It was awkward, but he managed to loosen his bindings.

A voice arose in the hall and Mr. Uriah and Merav, who hadn't yet agreed on any one particular word, stopped. The goons jerked to life. They made their way through the door. It wasn't long before two shots rang out and one of the men stumbled back into the room, his hand over his throat, blood thick and sluggish through his fingers.

Mr. Uriah removed a small pearl-handled, snub nose from his lap and pointed it at the hall. Saul used this opportunity to untie his legs. As he stood, Uriah aimed at him. Another shot rang in the hall.

"Who's the bigger threat?" Saul said.

Uriah faced the hall with his gun.

Saul went for the sword above the mantle. The grip had aged poorly, the wraps scratchy to the touch. The metal rasped coldly from the mount. Saul first cut the restraints from David and then Merav.

"See what you've brought upon us?" Uriah said.

Saul raised the blade to strike the old man, but Merav, still clumsy from the drug, managed to wedge herself between them.

"Even now?" Saul said.

"Even now."

Saul lowered the sword and turned to the hallway. He couldn't see anyone but heard footsteps. Pulling the corpse by the arms, he cleared the entryway. With his foot, he shut the door. Dumbstruck, Mr. Uriah's mouth fell agape. Saul grabbed Merav's chair and wedged it against the doorknob. Pulling the sword back into his hands, he turned around. Uriah's aim was back on him.

"Are you going to strike me down, Saul?"

"That's my intention."

"Please don't," Merav said. "None of us need to die."

"Merav, move away from him."

"I can't do that, Saul."

Angling the sword sideways, Saul tried to find an angle to strike. Each way he moved, Merav followed. "Then give me answers. No more riddles."

"David is right," Merav said, looking to the disheveled mess in the chair, drool hanging from his lip. "We needed an inside man. There were others. Potentials."

"Mindful of your place," Uriah said.

"We can't go on like this. We're at the end. It's all going to end tonight," she said.

Saul lowered the blade. There was honesty in Merav's face. A tension in the brow, a flex in the jaw. Some semblance of affection that he'd never recognized before. Whether she felt sorry for him, loved him, or had formed some sense of remorse he wasn't sure, but it was there. Silence held the room.

Merav began to speak again, "Saul, we needed you to stop Mr. Erelim. To stop the experiments."

"Why didn't you have me kill him earlier? Why drag this thing out?"

"We needed to find out who was in charge to remove the head," Mr. Uriah said.

"Erelim's head?" Saul said.

"Erelim is the head of the order. You're always so literal, Saul."

"Then what?"

Uriah shrugged.

Someone tried the door handle. They didn't force it. They didn't kick or shake it.

"Why me?"

"You were made for this," Saul.

"Made for what?"

"To kill."

"Did you select me at random?"

Merav shook her head. "No, we monitored you. You were one of a few prospects."

There were so many questions coming to him at once. Questions about the process of creating, of Uriah's vendetta, of the henchmen and the church and the group gathered in the dark firing guns, but the only thing that came out of his mouth was, "Do you love me?"

Merav's face went blank, then resurrected with a steely calm. If he didn't know better, he'd thought she was about to cry. "I'm sorry," she managed, her lips pulling thin against her teeth, the words darkened at the edges.

Saul's head was spinning, a weak thought lost in the whirlpool of moments. "Did you sleep with the other prospects?"

"Some."

"I'm done."

"You are not," Uriah answered.

"I'm not your tool."

"Now that you know what you are, you know they'll never stop hunting you. You'll kill Erelim before you'll let him take you."

"Let someone else do it."

"Who would that be, Saul?"

"There are others," Saul said, motioning towards David who seemed to be sobering.

Mr. Uriah eased his thin, chalky tongue over his lips and said, "David is all that is wrong with the project. When ideologues and spiritualists allow their agendas to obfuscate their data, they develop creatures like him. A mistake. But they're getting better at it. You, Saul, you are a streamlined hit man. A vast improvement. There is nothing wrong with you."

"You're wrong. There's more wrong with me than you know."

Uriah eased the gun into his lap, his sense of danger waning. "Now that they know you're working with us, they will come for you. Endlessly. They will come for you until they have you. Until they can strap you to a bed. Learn from you. Put you down when they have a new crop ready to test. You must understand that only I can protect you."

"And then what?" said Saul. "I kill when you need me and then you'll put me down? Deliver me from my design?"

The old man didn't answer, but it seemed the answer ghosted his face.

"I won't be your tool."

"Saul, you don't understand what you are. What you're born to. You'll keep killing. You will lust for it. It is the only thing that will bring you peace. Even after you do away with Erelim, you will crave the peace you find in the moments after you take a life."

Even as the words came and sat in Saul's stomach stony and cold, he found himself battling the urge to strike Uriah. This short waking life that began as a mystery, its petals an impossible labyrinth, where he found himself the keeper of a lexicon with no clear origin, where he wandered among a landscape of shadows in the valleys of a craggy skyline that only seemed to close in on him, had brought him no peace. If murder was the only thing that brought peace, perhaps he should do then what he was born to. He thought to fall on his own blade. End it. What then would Mr. Uriah do? Flipping the sword around, he looked first to Merav and then to Uriah, whose face slanted with a mixed sense of amusement and worry.

"You won't make sport of me," Saul said.

As if he could read Saul's thoughts, David said, "Don't do this, Saul. There's another way. We can go. Run."

Everyone looked to David. His interjection unexpected.

"Where would you go?" Uriah said. "To the alleys? To live like vermin? Stream along the gutters and feed on rubbish like a rat?"

"There's been enough death," David said.

Whether or not voices were guiding David to such clear thinking, Saul couldn't say, nor could he say if David had lived without killing, but it did seem to him that the looming dependency on murder would make his life a different game of chase. A game dictated by yearning, of pain and fixes. Maybe they could walk away. The city had a way of making a man feel as if there was no exit. No world outside of the looming towers and glassy storefronts. But maybe that was just perception for he could, after all, conjure up images of fields, beaches, mountains, and rivers.

"Let them go," Merav said.

"This is not your place," Mr. Uriah said.

"Let's leave, Saul," David said. He stood and stumbled back to the left of the door. He was having trouble righting himself. The drug hadn't completely worn off. Using the wall, he bent over and tried to collect himself.

"How many men are here, Uriah?" Saul said.

Uriah looked around and said, "Too many for you."

"That's untrue. We know that all but one are dead, for sure," Merav said. "Even if he's alive, I can get you safe passage. We can go to the station, put you on a train out of town."

They sat there in the quagmire of that thought, the four of them, the first honest balance since they'd joined, until the door began to shake in its frame and the chair threatened to give. It seemed to Saul there was no desirable outcome to the matter. To die one way was no better than the other. He would see how it'd play out. Let Uriah reap what he'd sewn. Saul kicked the chair free and stood to the right. For a time that seemed infinite but was surely but a few seconds, there was no sound and then a body emerged. An old man with brilliant white hair. Uriah's mouth opened and a dull sigh leaked from the hole in his throat.

23

AT FIRST, David couldn't see who was on the other side of the open door, only the faces of the others as they saw him enter. Mr. Uriah reached in his chair's compartments, searching for something, seemingly anything, but upon looking up, fell still again. Merav made to walk across the room but stopped mid-stride. Saul did nothing but stare. It was all a mystery to David, why the room had gone so still, but he understood it could mean nothing good. He slipped between the door and the wall. The voices began whispering to him. *It is God,* one said. *It is the man,* another said. A third claimed that Iosif had conjured a window into this moment and had come to free them. The more voices that arose, the less he could decipher until there was nothing but a pink noise of static.

Trying to regain his footing, David tried his best to recall what had happened. His mind was all fog and whispers. He'd awakened in a chair. On his left arm, a dried line of blood from his wound. On his right, a red welt from a restraint strapped too tightly. The room had been fuzzy; he had been focusing. There had been shapes in front of him. Ill-defined mounds lumbering in place, wavering and buoyant in the fog of his vision. The vertical shape had sprouted triangles, wings on his back. Then, as suddenly as they had appeared, they had receded. From its front, a thin, trembling line had emerged. To the right, there had been a more compact shape. Shadowed and still, it had erupted in movement as voices had arisen from the static of David's mind. The old man.

IN THE reflection of a glass cabinet, he saw the unmistakable glow of Erelim's hair. A ghost hovering in the shadows of the room.

"This," Erelim said, "is what I always knew it would come to. You and I meeting in the shadows. Somehow, though, I thought it would just be the two of us."

Uriah didn't reply. He clicked a button and his mechanical spider crawled over him. Releasing him from the pain, a moment of pleasure to clear his mind.

"I see you've outwitted David," Erelim said. "You call yourself Saul, correct?"

Saul seemed to think on this, to slip into a temporary pursuit of his name's origin before saying, "I'm no one."

"No One?"

"I've found naming things tiresome."

"Come with me, Saul. Do you mind that I call you Saul? No One is the name of a step-child sent to think about his actions in the corner."

Saul didn't reply.

"Saul, you're the survivor. The last of your siblings. Come to me. Let me show you the world we are building. You'll not suffer, I assure you."

"You promise I won't suffer but say nothing about death."

"I can't predict the future. Do you plan on dying? Is this something you desire?"

Saul didn't answer. He needled his fingertips in his palms.

"You've come so far, traveled the city in search of truth only to find mystery, to find death and duplicity, to watch those you befriend snatched from you, dealing death to those you encounter even when it's not at your hands. I will answer your questions. Lead you to that truth you seek with no ulterior motive. We just want to bring you back. To understand why you survived."

Saul weighed this, assessed the room. But his eyes moved in unnatural ways, a black ooze seeping from them, running in vines along his body and across the floor, slowly. Where were they going?

"If I go, will you spare the woman?"

"I cannot make that promise," Erelim said, "but I am interested in why you have concern about the outcome of one and not the other."

"Uriah's lucky I didn't kill him myself."

"You disappoint me, Saul. I thought you would know the difference between that which is real and that which is Maya. The ways of a woman are deceptive, the ways of the Order are honest."

Mr. Uriah, who'd been quiet up to this point, finally spoke. "You aim to tell us that the Order is more honest, yet you use those tools of man that you find most reprehensible. By using the fruits of his logic and metacognition, you believe you can remove these exact things from him. Do you honestly believe that creating a loyal servant to God justifies your means?"

"It is by God's grace, Uriah, that man has these tools at all."

David wanted to look around the door, to see the men talk. But terror held him, as he watched the onyx vines rooted in Saul's eyes spread, growing closer. Still, he listened, trying to decipher the conversation in the room from those in his head. It was growing more and more difficult to think about anything at all. How much could happen in his head before it burst open, a hail of grubs falling around his feet?

The vines were slithering. Moving toward him. *Lunge*, came a voice. *Destiny*, another. A third called out something he could not understand.

"There is no objectivity to your faith, Erelim. I know this better than anyone."

Erelim, moving into the room to the point where David saw the back of his head, the eerie glow of his unmovable hair, said, "Uriah, the Lord tests us. You have failed the test."

David looked to the floor to see that the vines were creeping onto his shoes. His body tingled with fear, felt almost weightless. From the cacophony of chatter, a voice, louder than the rest, began chanting. He pressed his hand against his temple. He tried to focus. What was the voice saying? It seemed to say, *home side yum*. Over and over. The others joined in. With each word Erelim spoke, the din of voices grew louder until the veins in his temples pounded against his fingers. He grew dizzy, the world losing definition. The vines began to lift, to rear their snake-like heads. His skin began to pepper with petechiae. He would choke, choke and explode. What was it they were telling him?

18

SAUL ATTEMPTED to hold Erelim's focus. Perhaps when Erelim was far enough inside the room, David could knock the gun from his hand.

Erelim pointed his gun at Merav. Saul stepped forward, but as he did, David emerged from the shadows and stabbed something into Erelim's neck. Initially, there was no blood. It looked as though the object had melded into Erelim's flesh, a dull indented seam joining the two. David pulled it free, exposing the biro, slicked red. Again he stabbed, this time deeper, blood from the carotid artery folded over his fingers. Stumbling forward, his body stiff with panic, Mr. Erelim tried to find language. At first his mouth could only fall into a terrible O. But after working at it a few times, he finally spoke. "How?"

David looked to his hand. The red, abject against his flesh.

"I don't know," David said. "I don't know."

He attempted to reach for the old man as he stepped forward in stupor. After several steps, the edge of Erelim's heel caught, and his body careened into Uriah's chair, tipping both men to the ground. Erelim curled his knees to his chest, and within a few minutes, minutes filled with desperate attempts at speech, his wild eyes went still and his body limp. They sat in silence, David shaking his head in a saddened state of shock as if the action was not of his design.

"Let's go," Merav said. "Now, before anyone else shows up."

Uriah, whose head hit the floor in a damp crunch, twitched. He was hurt but still alive. Saul grabbed the gun from Erelim and pointed it at Mr. Uriah.

"Please, Saul. Don't," Merav said, desperation weighing her lips at the corners.

Saul grabbed David by the wrist and they made their way to the elevator. As they waited for the lift, Saul noticed that the hotel had replaced the broken mirror in the hall with a painting of an old ship upon turbulent waters. Tempted, Saul pulled the painting back to see if they'd patched the holes. They had. After he lowered it, he fingered the gilded frame.

The elevator arrived. Saul looked through the window to ensure the operator was alone. He rested against the wall, his red hat tilted upon his head like some organ-grinder's monkey. Saul hid his gun. The boy opened the door and light filled the hall. He looked across their faces and then down to David's hand.

"Ain't you a sorry looking bunch?"

No one said a thing. They entered the elevator. Saul eyed the operator.

They descended in silence so thick it seemed as if it was pushing against the walls. David examined his wound in the brass, touching it and mouthing things. Saul tapped his foot against David's leg and he lowered his arms.

"You guys having some kind of celebration up there?"

"Something like that," Saul said.

"If it was anyone else, I guess Mr. Harman would'a kicked them out. Mr. Uriah must be pretty important."

"Mind your station," Merav said.

"Sorry, miss."

When the doors opened, Saul stepped out and gave the lobby a once over. He motioned for the others to follow. Merav took the lead. Saul turned to David and said, "Keep some pressure on that shoulder wound. We'll patch it up on the train."

David agreed.

They followed Merav through the city, the streetlights, small respites of life keeping the night from suffocating them, hovered like uncertain suns. Despite the turmoil, Merav's stature and stride was unchanged. Opaque lines streamed between the muscles in her calves as she hastened in impossibly sharp heels. How she avoided catching in the cracks of bricked roads, Saul couldn't understand. A skill a woman learned in life, he assumed. Then it hit—the pang that nothing with her was true. That she could, at that moment, be leading them to some other mystery, to some lab or apartment or an alley filled with murder-eyed men. What then? he wondered. Would he plug her full of bullets? The idea cut him two ways. The desire to see the lovely tendrils of crimson pinstripe her pale flesh, to hear her last gasp. The horror of knowing that she was no longer in the world. The latter was almost too much to bear. Despite her duplicity, she was the only pleasure he knew, even if she wasn't his. Even if she was like the full moon, a ghostly body falling into men's lives endlessly but never landing. Ever changing but never her own light.

David busied himself with those inner voices. He looked to his skin, picked at his arms, and whispered answers. Perhaps, with time, Saul would understand what accelerated his episodes, but he hoped not to find out, to disappear into the fabric of some other place once the train traveled far enough. In his head, he had images of the west, grand painted sunsets dipping behind amber plateaus, but he couldn't be sure such a place existed, or that anything existed on the opposite side of the city.

Every noise roused him from his thoughts. A cab backfiring, a bus opening its doors, two homeless men fighting outside a liquor store. When they passed the city amphitheater, David stared at the vacant lot behind it, watching the litter blow and smack against trees and poles. He chewed on a word, something round.

"There's nothing there," Saul said.

"I know," David said, a sadness in his voice thick as a cold.

There were no more henchmen in the shadows. No strangers with guns looming to attack along the way. Only the dying hustle of a destination city. Outside the train station, a small group of businessmen gathered in gray suits and tan trench coats. They spoke of numbers and objects and boomed laughter. It wouldn't have surprised Saul if one turned and fired, but they didn't.

At the ticket booth, Merav rang a bell. A man with a gray beard and thin metal-framed glasses came to the window and slid a small section of glass open.

"What do you need, lady?"

"I need two one-way tickets."

"To where?"

"The end of the line."

"There's no city with that name."

Merav opened an envelope filled with bills. She pulled several out and said, "As far as the next train goes. If that's not far enough, then get them the next connecting lines."

The man opened a thick, leather bound book and flipped through it. He examined it over the top ridge of his glasses. "How 'bout the 23? It'll take you to the coast? Any further, you'd need a boat."

"That will do nicely," Merav said and paid the man. When he attempted to hand her change, she shook her head and said, "If anyone asks, you never sold these tickets."

The bearded man opened his mouth as if to speak, said nothing, and handed her the tickets. He gave her directions to platform five and asked her to come again.

Among the lofty arches of the station, pigeons flew between beams, cooing and shitting. Staring up at them, David stumbled next to Saul, who'd taken a hold of David's arm to keep him on course. Merav scarcely turned and looked at them. They passed the locker where he'd found the photograph and Saul wondered if this was something that had happened before. He stopped and asked them to wait. Slipping a coin into the locker, he opened it, pulled the photo from his breast pocket, slipped it inside, and entered the same combination he'd used before.

The train was waiting at the platform, its engine hissing. The others were already on board, awaiting the departure. Merav gave the tickets to the attendant of the Luxury car. She turned to them and said, "This is it, boys."

"David, go on. I'll join you in a couple minutes."

David looked confused, lost, as if his thoughts had become so minor in his head that he was unable to find the cabin on his own. The attendant took notice and said, "Sir, I'll show you to your cabin."

Merav's eyes seemed to bulge, more lovely and radiant than ever before. "Your eyes," he managed. "They—"

"Don't flatter me, Saul. It's a dead end."

"Right."

"You need to board."

"Merav, you can come with us. Leave this puzzle behind."

"You know better."

"If I did, I wouldn't ask."

"There's nothing here for you, Saul." Merav bit the inside of her lip, some tic she'd likely never known about.

She began to back away and Saul pulled her to him, kissed her. She didn't part lips. They remained hard drawn and cold. Releasing her, he said, "Sure. Sure."

"Goodbye, Saul."

23

THE LANDSCAPE seemed to roll by with leisure. Saul gazed out the window in a manner that seemed as if he might be building the world, considering which tree would come zipping past the window next. David had managed spots of sleep here and there, enough to dim the voices, but not enough to silence them. Although he knew the names of many things passing outside the window, he didn't know why. *Evergreen, River, Bridge, Cow, Tractor, Barn.* The further west they traveled, the colder it grew outside. A patchwork of frost gathered along the rounded corners of the cabin windows. He touched it, melting a clear oval into the nearly opaque patch. This pleased him at first but soon he felt the cold run along the edge of his femur, through the meat of his muscles, and warp around his lungs. David inhaled and held his breath to warm them.

"You're fine," Saul said without looking.

"Sometimes I get cold," David said.

"Sometimes we all get cold. Grab a blanket."

David sat blinking. "A blanket?"

"Shit, David," Saul said, standing and pulling a blanket from a cabinet. He spread it into the air with a flick and laid it upon David. He'd not had a blanket in longer than he could remember. What had he become? He thought of Uriah.

"Do you think I'm a mutt?"

"No."

"What are we? I mean, are we human?"

"Did you bleed?"

"Yeah."

"Then you're human."

David looked out the window and, upon seeing a cow, said, "A cow's not human."

"What?"

"A cow bleeds. It's not human."

"Goddamn it, David. I don't know what we are. We're a couple guys been beat to hell, that's all I know."

"I was scared to fall asleep."

"Why?"

"Thought I'd wake up in that place I dream about. The place with the tubs. The doctor who speaks in sharp words I don't understand."

"German."

"German?"

"Yes, German."

"I don't speak German."

"I don't know if I do or not. I know he's German, though. I dreamed of him, too. I never saw his face in my dreams but I saw it when I went to that place. How long did you sleep, anyway? Every time I woke up, you were awake."

"I don't sleep much. It's why I hear the voices."

Saul adjusted himself in his seat and said, "What are the voices?"

223

"They talk to me. Tell me to do things. Sometimes they're good and sometimes they're bad. Like they tell me about the maggots and I start picking or cutting my skin."

"You can't tell it's not real?"

"No."

"Have they always been there?"

"Only when I don't sleep." David thought about Ileana. "But since I woke in that room, I've only had one decent night's sleep. When I met the carnival people."

"What about when Uriah knocked you out?"

"It was worse when I woke up. The voices. Whatever he used."

Saul stood up and looked through the compartments. He found a large brimmed dress hat and put it on. After some fussing, he looked at his reflection in the mirror and sat down. Pushing the brim down in front, Saul eased back into the seat, leaned against the window and tuned out. David needled the warm blanket with his fingers. He wondered if his new future would contain beds and blankets, if he might find sleep with these comforts. He lay upon the bench and tried to sleep. In the trembling black of his eyelids, the memories of the previous day began to arise. As if he'd not even been present, he watched his hand stab a pen into Erelim's neck, the blood spraying out in a mist. This wasn't him but something else. Some chaotic force in him, in the universe. That force that turned dogs mad and men murderous. Something innate in the universe, perhaps. Some x-factor that neither faith nor science could locate. A voice hissed to him, then. *Look*, it said. *Look at them feast*. David did not. He squeezed his eyelids tighter together. Those hungry mouths. The itch began to build until he felt as if he might burst into flames. He began to pick at his bandages.

"If you keep that up," Saul said, "I'll kill you where you lay."

The brim of the hat hid much of Saul's face, but he wasn't smiling.

"Why do you think we were all called David and not Adam?"

Saul said, "I imagine it's because David was a warrior and Adam was a fuck-up."

"Do you think we're really killers?" David said.

"I don't know, David. You might not be."

"Are you?"

"I've killed and enjoyed it. I guess that means I am."

"I've killed, too," David said.

"Did you enjoy it?"

"No."

"Then I suppose you're not a killer. Just a man who did what needed doing."

"Thanks, Saul."

"For what?"

"For saying that."

"Sure."

"Saul?"

"I will kill you, David. Let me sleep."

David looked at Saul's hands. Watched them twitch when he grew angry. He believed Saul. He would kill him if pushed to it. David remained silent for a long time. The sun was lost to some other part of the world and then resurrected on the other side of the train some time later. It broke the ridgeline, burning through the barren trees. He'd not remembered seeing it so bright before, so free from the smog that held the city captive.

David had to use the bathroom but feared waking Saul. He held it until Saul roused and said he was going to grab breakfast in the dining car. When he returned, he brought David a glass of warm milk mixed with cinnamon and chamomile and a small tablet. He said he'd gotten the pill from an Indian woman who took them because she had trouble sleeping on trains.

"What is it?"

"Valerian. All natural."

David swallowed the pill and drank the milk, finding it too herby to enjoy. They sat in silence and David fell to sleep. He dreamed of Ileana walking down a long flight of stairs, a radiant sparkling ruby dress traipsing behind her. It was completely silent. She spoke but he couldn't hear her voice. He tried to speak but found himself mute. She continued to walk toward him. A baby carriage rolled past her. People rushed around in panic. A woman at the top of the steps screamed as she watched the baby roll toward the street, her howl, quiet at first, grew louder and louder until he awoke to the shriek of the train.

"You slept for a while," Saul said.

Outside, the sky was washed pink and yellow, the clouds shadowing at their bottoms. "I missed the day," David said.

"Do you hear voices?"

"No."

Saul looked out the window. "We're nearly there."

"How do you know?"

"I saw a seagull."

An hour later buildings began to occur with greater frequency. First, there were farmhouses, then mills and factories, finally track homes and clusters of shops. When the train began to slow, David was surprised to find that no buildings surrounding the station were over three stories tall. There were no vagrants lining the streets, no litter clinging to the curbs. The streets were wide and not overrun with tourists and business people. A family of five rode bikes down a well-lit street. He'd never seen a family riding bikes. It struck him as a good omen. That the world beyond the train doors would offer more than dumpsters and whispers.

"This is us," Saul said.

"What do we do now?"

"We part ways. I go my way. You go yours."

The space outside was oppressive in a new way. Exposing. It was not lost on Saul. "Look," he said, "you can tag along for a while. I'll help you get settled and then we can separate." He reached into the inside pocket of his jacket. "We've got some money from Uriah. It'll last awhile."

"Thank you."

"Just don't make me regret it," Saul said.

David began folding the blanket. He thought to put it back, but rolled it up and slipped it beneath his arm.

"There'll be blankets where we lay," Saul said.

"This one," David said, looking at it and then feeling foolish for his sentimentality. He lowered it, but before he could drop it on the seat, Saul said, "I get it. Bring it."

Saul smiled at him. He had a poor smile, as if he'd never smiled before. Saul left the cabin and walked down the hall toward the exit. David did a once over, then he watched families and friends greet the arriving passengers with hugs and handshakes on the platform. How nice that must be. To have a family outside of his fallen brothers who found life in a hotel room. A burst of steam rose from the train and the mass of people was obscured by a deep gray fog. Through it, a luminous white mass of hair emerged and moved to the right. David's body ran cold, his hands itched with fear. By the time the steam had cleared, the man had vanished. Saul came to the door.

"What's the hold up?"

"I think I saw—" David began, but his thoughts were interrupted by a whispering voice inside him—*Nothing*.

"You saw what?"

"Nothing," David said.

Saul placed his hand on David's shoulder and they walked away. They stepped off the train and wandered through the beach town until they came upon an upscale hotel. Saul requested adjoining rooms with an ocean view. When they stood at their respective doors, Saul told David to knock three times on his wall if anything should happen. "Tomorrow," Saul said, "we'll get sorted."

When David entered his room, he walked to the window and sat on the ledge for a time. It had never occurred to him that there could be something so open as the ocean. Even during those last moments of light, he could see for miles. The horizon only punctuated by the occasional ship, distant and small. The division of sky and sea was nearly indistinguishable, both blue and seemingly infinite. In the morning, he would walk along the beach. Let the air fill his lungs. He would touch the water. Raise a finger to his lips. Taste the salt.

When the sun finally dipped behind the ocean, David undressed and crawled between the clean sheets. They were cool and crisp. David lay in his bed listening to the faint rush of waves hitting the beach. It calmed him. The moon was bright and he could see craters he'd never noticed before. He fell to sleep and dreamed of the moon as a luminous head growing larger and larger until the world was crushed beneath it.

END

about duncan b. barlow

Before writing, duncan b. barlow was a touring musician who played with Endpoint, By The Grace of God, Guilt, the aasee lake, The Lull Account, Good Riddance, and many more. His interviews about music and subculture have been published in academic texts, books, and magazines such as: *Straight Edge: Clean-Living Youth, Hardcore Punk, and Social Change* on Rutgers University Press, and *We Owe You Nothing: Punk Planet Collected Interviews* on Akashic., and *Burning Fight* on Revelation Records. His other books include *Super Cell Anemia* and *Of Flesh and Fur*. His work has appeared in *The Denver Quarterly, The Collagist, Banango Street, Calamari Press, The Apeiron Review, Meat for Tea,* and *Masque and Spectacle*. He teaches creative writing and publishing at The University of South Dakota, where he is publisher at Astrophil Press and the managing editor at *South Dakota Review*. He has also edited for *Tarpaulin Sky*, and *The Bombay Gin*, among others.

www.duncanbbarlow.com

CPSIA information can be obtained
at www.ICGtesting.com
Printed in the USA
LVOW12s1832060417
529885LV00003B/547/P